SPECIAL MESSAGE TO READERS

THE ULVERSCROFT FOUNDATION
(registered UK charity number 264873)
was established in 1972 to provide funds for
research, diagnosis and treatment of eye diseases.
Examples of major projects funded by
the Ulverscroft Foundation are:-

- The Children's Eye Unit at Moorfields Eye
  Hospital, London
- The Ulverscroft Children's Eye Unit at Great
  Ormond Street Hospital for Sick Children
- Funding research into eye diseases and
  treatment at the Department of Ophthalmology,
  University of Leicester
- The Ulverscroft Vision Research Group,
  Institute of Child Health
- Twin operating theatres at the Western
  Ophthalmic Hospital, London
- The Chair of Ophthalmology at the Royal
  Australian College of Ophthalmologists

You can help further the work of the Foundation
by making a donation or leaving a legacy.
Every contribution is gratefully received. If you
would like to help support the Foundation or
require further information, please contact:

THE ULVERSCROFT FOUNDATION
The Green, Bradgate Road, Anstey
Leicester LE7 7FU, England
Tel: (0116) 236 4325

website: www.foundation.ulverscroft.com

NO PEACE FOR A REBEL

The Civil War over, retired soldier Ethan Cole joins a group led by his former major, Daniel Reno, unaware that he's being drawn into a plot that could change the course of history. Believing he owes Reno his life, he goes along with the major's plan to stage a gold bullion robbery. But later, when Cole learns that Reno has a sinister goal in mind, he tries to prevent a war — and a vicious showdown with a former friend.

PETER WILSON

NO PEACE FOR A REBEL

Complete and Unabridged

LINFORD
Leicester

First published in Great Britain in 2012 by
Robert Hale Limited
London

First Linford Edition
published 2013
by arrangement with
Robert Hale Limited
London

LP

A catalogue record for this book is available
from the British Library.

ISBN 978–1–4448–1709–6

Published by
F. A. Thorpe (Publishing)
Anstey, Leicestershire

Set by Words & Graphics Ltd.
Anstey, Leicestershire
Printed and bound in Great Britain by
T. J. International Ltd., Padstow, Cornwall

This book is printed on acid-free paper

Prologue

The general felt all of his 58 years as he stroked his grey beard and collected his thoughts. Then, as though suddenly satisfied that the time really had come, he sat at the desk, took up his pen and began to write.

He dated it 10 April 1865 and addressed it to his troops. It read:

> After four years of arduous service marked by unsurpassed courage and fortitude, the army of North Virginia has been compelled to yield to overwhelming numbers and presences. I need not tell the survivors of so many hard fought battles who have remained steadfast to the last that I have consented to this result from no distrust of them. But feeling that valour and

1

devotion could accomplish nothing that would compensate for the loss that would attend the continuance of the contest I determined to avoid the useless sacrifice of those whose past services have endeared them to their countrymen. By the terms of the agreement, officers and men can return to their homes and remain until exchanged. You will take with you the satisfaction that consciousness of duty faithfully performed and I earnestly pray that a merciful God will extend His blessing and protection.

With an increasing admiration of your constancy and devotion to your country and a grateful remembrance of your kind and generous consideration for myself I bid you all an affectionate farewell.

R.E. Lee

Good Friday, April 15th. Abraham Lincoln was assassinated. Andrew Johnson succeeded but could not control vengeful radical Republicans and a harsh bitter period followed. Unjust rules were imposed on the old Confederacy and there was much bitterness and defiant pride from the white Southerners, leading eventually to the formation of the Ku Klux Klan.

1

Tennessee, Spring 1866.

Ethan Cole reached for his gun but he was too slow.

'Bang! Bang!'

Ethan clutched his chest and slumped dramatically to his knees.

'You — you sure got me this time, pardner,' he gasped before buckling over and rolling on to his back.

Next instant he was staring up into the round, smiling face of his 6-year-old nephew. He returned the smile and reached up to grab the boy, pulling him to the ground.

'You win again, little Jonathan. You're too quick for me.'

Getting to his feet, he released the youngster, dusting them both down.

'Now it's time for you to run along for your supper — and don't tell your ma we've been shooting each other. She wouldn't like that.'

'They're only toy guns, Uncle Ethan,' the boy protested. 'They're not real.'

Cole got to his feet and finished dusting himself down. But one day they will be real, he thought, and that day will come too soon.

'You coming for supper, too, Uncle?' the boy asked, shaking off the last of the dust.

Cole put his arm around the boy's shoulder. 'Tell your mother I'll be along later. Got some tidying up to do in the store first. Now off you go.'

He slapped the boy playfully on the backside and watched him run off towards the little house at the end of Main Street. Jonathan was his brother's son but Matthew was dead, another statistic among the many thousands of victims of the four brutal years that Ethan believed would remain a scar on the country's history.

Ethan had been one of the lucky ones, escaping with nothing more serious than a few scratches from falling off his horse and a flesh wound from a stray Union bullet. His brother had died in his arms to bring home all the horrors of a war that the South could never win.

But the war had ended a year ago. Southern Tennessee was slowly adapting to the new order and Ethan's life as a soldier was behind him. It had been buried alongside his younger brother. The job of small-town storekeeper would not have suited many of his fellow officers but he was happy to leave his guns and stained grey uniform locked away in a back room trunk. Here in Clarkston he was among friends and family. Young Jonathan and his mother were now that family. And he owed them.

Walking slowly back into his store, Ethan wondered what Alice would be serving up for supper. She was a fine cook, a good mother and he was not alone in thinking she was a beautiful woman. He looked forward to his occasional evening meals at the little house far more than he dared to admit to himself.

Alice was his brother's widow. They had been married for five years before the war dragged Matthew away from home. It had been Ethan's duty to report that his brother had been killed in one of the last actions of the conflict. The Battle of Five Forks southwest of Petersburg, Virginia, on the first day of April a year ago had signalled the beginning of the end and triggered the retreat that led to the rebels' surrender a week later.

Alice had cried on his shoulder long and hard when he delivered the news that Matthew had been killed. He had offered the best comfort he could and never once had she raised the subject which must have pained her most.

It had been Ethan who had persuaded the younger Cole to join him in the fight for the Confederate cause. Even now, more than a year after that fateful battle, Ethan Cole's conscience troubled him.

Why had he talked young Matthew into joining the Southern army? He was a family man with a young son hardly old enough to walk, a loving wife and the prospects of a comfortable if uneventful life as sheriff of a small town in his home state of Tennessee.

Ethan knew the answer without indulging in too much soul-searching. It had been a selfish act of a jealous older man. He wanted his brother at his side but worse than that, he was jealous of Matthew, his family . . . and especially his wife. Simple, selfish jealousy.

He shrugged off the growing feeling that occasionally returned to haunt him and went to the back of the store to finish his daily chores. By the time they were done those feelings of guilt would have disappeared.

He knew nothing of the man who stood outside the saloon and studied the young boy playing pretend gun-fighters with his uncle. The stranger watched the boy run off towards the house at the end of the street before dropping the remains of his half-smoked cigar and crushing it under his heel. He looked both ways along the street before crossing to head for the general store. It was time to break up this blissful state of happy family. Ethan Cole's idyllic world was about to be shattered.

2

Frank Mason washed and shaved only when the mood took him and he had done neither for four days. The ride to this godforsaken place they called Clarkston had been hot and long and with each day Mason's notorious short temper was stretched to its limit more than once until he was ready to challenge the most innocent glance from a stranger.

He told himself that if Cole turned out to be a problem he would probably ignore his orders and shoot the bastard where he stood.

Ethan Cole, the blue-eyed boy in the grey uniform, a small-town storekeeper. Mason almost laughed aloud. Did Reno really need somebody who was nothing more than a nursemaid to a 6-year-old kid?

Mason checked his gun-belt — a

habit he had developed long before the war — and climbed the steps leading into the Clarkston General Store.

★   ★   ★

Ethan was carrying a sack of coffee when he spotted the tall, slim figure silhouetted in the doorway. It was too dark to make out the features but the stooping stance of the stranger was vaguely familiar.

'Good evening, Captain.'

The voice was harsh, coarsened by too much whiskey and tobacco. And again he thought it sounded familiar.

Ethan dropped the sack on to the counter and crossed to the centre of the store. The visitor's features came slowly into focus and Ethan's heart sank. It was a face he hoped he would never see again.

'Mason!'

The man stepped inside and offered his version of a friendly smile.

'The very same, Captain. Trooper

Frank Mason. Though I ain't sure about you being a captain no more. I ain't never seen a captain wearing an apron.'

'The war's over, Frank. Has been for a year. Maybe you haven't heard.'

Mason snorted his disgust. 'Not for everyone it ain't.'

Ethan picked up the sack and carried it to the back of the counter.

'So what is it you want, Frank? Or maybe you are just passing through?'

He knew that if Frank Mason had anything to say he was going to say it without any encouragement but he was in a hurry. He had a supper date with Alice and young Jonathan.

'The major sent me,' Mason said at last.

Ethan ignored him but he knew this was a visit he had feared ever since the signing of the surrender by Robert E. Lee at Appomattox back in April of the previous year. The signing had officially ended four years of bloody conflict but signatures on a piece of paper could not

12

wipe out the bitterness that had festered and grown with every battle and every death. Then the assassination of Abraham Lincoln by Southern fanatic John Wilkes Booth just five days later confirmed that the hatreds of war lingered on.

Lincoln's promise of a conciliatory peace for the secessionist states died with him and the South became the target for corrupt state governments eager for revenge.

Ethan knew all this but the following year had gradually eased much of the pain and the hate. But not for everybody.

'You hear me, Cole?' Gone was the mockingly polite 'Captain'.

'I hear you, Frank, but I'm not listening.'

Mason's chuckle was humourless.

'The major reckoned that's what you would say,' he said reaching inside his shirt. He withdrew a long brown envelope and tossed it on to the counter. 'He said you might need some persuading so he told me to give you that. Read it, Cole. I'll be waiting in the saloon across the street. You've got one hour and then . . . '

He allowed his voice to tail off and he turned and left the store. Ethan watched him go before picking up the envelope, thumbing it open and unfolding the contents.

My Dear Ethan
You will be surprised to hear from your old major after all this time and probably even more surprised that I have sent Frank Mason with this message, knowing as I do that you did not part on the best of terms. However I felt Mason was the ideal person to convey the seriousness of this request — I am reluctant to use the word 'order' to a trusted comrade — and he is not the sort to take a refusal, should you consider that an option.
You will remember, my friend, the pledge we made in that darkest

hour at the crossroads of Peters-
burg when we were scattered to the
four winds. Sadly it was the night
that your brother was killed, unlike
the day at Knox County in '63
when I was only able to save you
thanks to a stroke of God's good
fortune as he smiled on the
righteous of the day.

Ethan paused to reflect on the
major's flowery prose which he recognized and left him in no doubt that the
letter in his hands was the genuine
article from the man who had been his
commander and had indeed saved his
life.

The conflict may have been offi-
cially over for almost a year but
there are those of like minds —
and I know I can include you
among them, my friend — who
believe that Lee's surrender was
nothing short of treachery of so
many brave men. Subsequent

15

actions by Washington confirm this beyond doubt but now we have the opportunity to redress some of the balance. I know I can trust you to follow Mason and his men who will lead you to where we are based. I must stress that time is short and the need for discretion has never been more important. Remember that pledge, Captain: 'When the call comes I will answer it'. This is that call. For your own safety and that of your family — you have a young nephew and his widowed mother to think about — I am leaving you to do the right thing.

Be here, soon, my friend.

Major Daniel Reno.

Ethan screwed up the letter into a ball and hurled it across the room. What in God's name did Reno expect of him? Did he really expect him to abandon everything and come running to his side after all this time? Many soldiers from both sides made pledges during times of crisis but those days were behind them. It was time to embrace peace.

But could he simply turn his back on the man who had saved his life? Ethan removed the apron that Mason had mocked, rolled down his sleeves and prepared to lock up the store. The letter had revealed nothing of what his former major was planning. He had to know more and maybe Mason had some of the answers.

Striding out, he crossed the street and entered the saloon. A group of card players occupied one table but Mason stood alone at the bar. He turned as Ethan pushed open the batwings and a crooked smile crossed his face.

'You're a quick learner, Captain,' Mason sneered. 'I gave you an hour and here you are. We've still got time for a drink or two.'

'No drinks, Frank,' Ethan said bitterly. 'I'm not here for that. I want some answers.'

Mason turned away to retrieve his glass. He eyed Ethan closely. He had never really liked Cole, never got to know him. He was the old major's pet captain and far too fond of doing his soldiering according to the book for Mason's liking. War was a bloody business and you made up your own rules. Cole had no stomach for the dirty jobs. He left those to men like Mason. Yet Cole took all the credit — him and his brother. Too bad he got shot up.

Frank Mason emptied and then refilled his whiskey glass.

'You read the major's letter. Ain't that enough for you?'

Ethan thought about that before answering. Daniel Reno's letter had explained nothing but it was doubtful if the major would have entrusted Frank Mason with any information.

Mason downed his whiskey in one gulp and slammed the glass on to the bar.

'Look, Cole, I've been sent here to

18

get you because the major said so. Now, if that ain't good enough for you I've got other orders. Either way, I don't care.'

'What other orders, Frank?'

Mason's oily grin revealed tobacco-stained teeth.

'You don't suppose I came all this way alone just to be told you got something better to do than come when the major calls. I'll make it easy for you, Captain. The others are camped a couple of miles outside of town and if we're not there by sundown, they've got their orders to come and find us.'

He paused to pour himself another drink giving Ethan time to take in the message. And there was no doubt that the message was far more than that — it was a threat.

'Is that supposed to frighten me, Frank?' he asked at length. 'You should know that I don't scare easily.'

'Naw,' Mason drawled. 'Maybe you don't. But remember I'm only passing on what the major told me would happen if you didn't like what was in his letter. 'Get Cole here and do what it takes. If he still won't come, then . . . ' he left the rest up to me and the boys. He told me that you would have a young widow woman and her kid to think about. He stressed that. Reckoned when you remembered that you'd come along quiet enough.'

Instinctively, Ethan clenched his fists. He felt the anger rising inside him and he had to fight the sudden urge to lash out and smash Mason's sneering face to a bloody pulp. But far worse than the surge of anger was the stomach-churning feeling that Mason — and that meant Major Reno — was threatening his family.

Daniel Reno had saved his life during the war, and he had tried to save Matthew. Why was he now sending his henchman to issue warnings and threats?

Lashing out at Mason would not help. Ethan knew that the only way to get to the bottom of this was to go with him; to see Daniel face to face. He couldn't believe that the man who had saved his life would now be threatening to destroy it. Whatever the major was planning had to be important and he obviously needed Ethan Cole.

Without another word to Mason he turned and left the saloon and headed for the house. But there would be no happy family supper tonight.

* * *

Ethan hugged his young nephew and turned to face the boy's mother.

She had been understandably withdrawn ever since he broke the news that he would be leaving them for a few days. But it was not the simple announcement that he would be out of town that had caused Alice to go into an uneasy quiet. It was the presence of Ethan's saddle-bag and gun-belt on the table that worried her into silence. He had said precious little of the reasons

21

for leaving town other than to tell them both that he would return 'in a few days'.

But why the guns? And what was in the bag?

Young Jonathan, however, was full of questions and Ethan felt a twinge of guilt at the deception he engineered by telling the boy that he was only visiting an old army friend.

He released the boy and forced a smile for the boy's mother.

'I promise, I'll be back as soon as I can. I don't know why Reno wants to see me but it must be important for him to send Frank Mason looking for me. Don't worry . . . ' he checked himself. How could he tell her how he felt? She had been married to his brother; they had known each other since they were children. Now was not the time.

He kissed her lightly on the forehead and playfully ruffled the boy's hair. Alice watched him walk away towards the saloon where he had hitched his horse. Jonathan stood at her side but did not see the tear in his mother's eye.

★　★　★

The four riders dismounted and led their horses single file along the narrow ridge that dropped steeply into the valley. It was a dark night and the moon offered only occasional light with its infrequent appearances from behind the heavy clouds.

Mason led the line with Ethan close behind. The others, whose names Cole neither knew nor cared to know, brought up the rear. Both were short, stocky men in their late thirties and although he had a vague recollection of having met them before he had no inclination to confirm the assumption. As far as he was concerned they were two hired guns doing as they were told, whether it was by Frank Mason or Daniel Reno.

The moon put in another brief appearance as the four reached the end of the narrow track and stepped out on to the wide valley floor. They remounted and urged their horses into a steady trot. Mason had offered no information about their eventual destination but Ethan was not inclined to ask. He would discover soon enough. In the meantime the four maintained their strained, hostile silence broken only by grumbles from the pair at the rear.

It was just before dawn and they had slowed their mounts to a gentle walking pace when Mason broke into Ethan's thoughts.

'You're a quiet one, Captain. Maybe you're worried she might find somebody else to keep your bed warm while you're away?'

Ethan remained silent.

'She's a pretty thing, your brother's woman, and that's a fact. If I was you I'd sure be mad at the major for dragging me away from a woman like that.' He turned in his saddle. 'What do you say, boys?'

The two men at the back laughed in approval.

'I'd be mad as hell, Frank,' one of them cackled. 'Maybe if the captain here don't make it back we could fill in for him. What do you think, Dutch?'

The man called Dutch laughed, a hoarse, grating laugh.

'Sounds like the lady won't be short of company,' Mason sneered. 'And if — ' He got no further.

Ethan's self-restraint snapped. Leaping from his saddle, he hurled himself at the taller man and the pair crashed to the ground in an untidy heap. The impact knocked the wind out of Mason but Ethan, the pent-up anger releasing itself in a burst of hatred, dragged him to his feet.

Releasing all the fury that had built up inside him, Ethan smashed his fist into the other man's face and sent him spinning backwards into a nearby bush. He didn't wait for Mason to get to his feet. Instead, he launched himself forward into the darkness. The two men grappled among the shrubbery before Ethan pulled Mason up and spun him round, hurling him against his horse, causing the animal to rear up and gallop into the distance.

The pair rolled over and Ethan felt the full force of Mason's knee in his groin. Gasping for breath, he lashed out with a punch that caught Mason on the side of the temple but it did no damage. They rolled apart and in the semi-darkness, Ethan saw Mason reach for his gun. It wasn't there; it was lying somewhere out of harm's way deep in the shrubbery. Panicking, Mason launched himself forward, his fingers groping for Ethan's face, searching for the eyes. But Ethan was too quick for him, rolling aside and delivering a vicious punch to the stomach that doubled up the cursing adversary.

They scrambled to their feet and slugged it out toe-to-toe, Ethan getting the warm taste of blood as Mason's flying fist caught him full on the mouth.

Above them, still motionless in their

saddles, Dutch and the man with no name leaned silently on their saddle horns.

This was not their business. It was a private matter and they were not being paid enough to interfere. The major's orders had been clear enough: bring in Ethan Cole. Like them, Frank Mason was just the hired help. His well-being was no concern of theirs. They were more than happy to watch the two men spill blood.

They would happily pick up the pieces when it was all over.

For several minutes Cole and Mason whipped up their mutual hatred into a frenzy of brutal savagery. It ended suddenly. Ethan hit the other with a swinging left fist that caught him flush on the jaw. He stood over the stricken man and waited for him to get to his feet. Instead Mason just lay there motionless.

Wiping the blood from his battered and swollen face, Ethan barked an order to the two men.

'Get him on his feet. Tie him in his saddle if you have to.' Down to his left a weak groan told him that Mason was coming round. He had taken one hell of a beating.

Ethan walked away to retrieve the horse that had run off during the fight. The struggle had taken a lot out of him but it had also focused his mind on something he had chosen to hide for more than a year. His feelings for Alice went far deeper than the natural concern for a dead brother's young widow and her son.

Taking the loose reins, he led the stray horse back to the others. Mason had been helped up on to his mount and was sitting hunched miserably in his saddle.

Ethan climbed up on to his horse and looked closely at the bruised and battered figure.

'Count yourself lucky, Frank,' he said quietly. 'Cross me again . . . and I'll kill you.'

He turned his horse and went to the

rear of the group. He had no intention of turning his back on any of this trio until they had reached their destination, and maybe not even then.

He was eager to hear why Daniel Reno had sent a group of hoodlums to collect him when a telegraph or a visit in person would have achieved the same result.

3

The waist had thickened and the jowls were heavier but the tall, silver-haired moustachioed man was still an imposing figure as he strode purposefully across the main street towards the courthouse. He nodded politely and smiled when two of the town's prominent Women's Committee greeted him. They knew a gentleman when they saw one and Daniel Reno was the perfect gentleman in any company. Everywhere the streets were bustling with the good folk of Knoxville going about their business but his focus was on other more pressing matters. His concern was in the courtroom where his one-time colleague was facing the judge. Whatever the charge — and Reno had not taken time to familiarize himself with the details — he was fairly certain that the verdict would be guilty.

Irishman Martin Rafferty, with a fiery temper to match his red hair and ruddy complexion, was not a stranger to the ways of the courts of Tennessee. His drunken, foul-mouthed and often violent behaviour had regularly landed him in trouble with the law to be followed by a brief, mainly overnight, detention in the cells.

Occasionally Rafferty would take his high spirits too far and tested the patience of the courts following a night of excessive drinking and violence that merited more than a mere one night's denial of liberty.

As he mounted the courthouse steps and sidled along the back wall of the room to avoid any unwanted attention, former Confederate Army Major Daniel Reno sincerely hoped that the hot-headed Irishman had avoided any such serious incidents on this occasion. He needed Rafferty sober and free for at least the next four days.

Reno slid into a vacant seat and

listened while a man he recognized as a local trader gave his evidence against Rafferty who stood, hunched and disconsolate, clearly attempting to persuade the judge of his contrition, waiting for the inevitable.

The witness, a weak, frail figure who kept glancing towards Rafferty as though the Irishman were about to pounce on him at any moment, muttered his evidence like a man frightened of his own shadow. That shadow, Reno realized, was the buxom, sour-faced woman among the public spectators: his wife.

There were bursts of laughter as the man explained how Rafferty, drunk as usual, entered his wife's ladies' emporium and began trying on various items of women's clothing, dresses and hats, ignoring the privacy of the female customers as he danced and tunelessly sang his way through the racks of clothes.

'Sure, it was only a bit of fun, Your Honour,' Rafferty interrupted loudly. 'I'd just won a few dollars at the cards and I wanted to treat my fiancée.

'I thought a nice dress and hat would do the trick to . . . well, you know, persuade my intended to . . . er well you know.'

More laughter from the spectators only strengthened the judge's resolve and caused Reno to sigh in despair.

'Mr Rafferty, you have no fiancée. No woman in her right mind would promise to marry such a vagabond as yourself and your idea of fun appears to appeal to nobody but yourself.'

'Aw, sir, sure I can't be all bad. I've said I'm sorry to the lady and offered to pay for any damage I may have caused. Is that not a sign that I am truly an honourable man?'

Even the judge — and Reno — raised a smile at that.

'If you had not appeared before this court on at least five previous occasions I might be tempted to believe you. However, I find the case of vandalism, wilful damage, drunkenness and anything else you might like to mention, to be proven and since putting you in jail appears to have no effect on your lawless Irish character, I order you to pay one hundred dollars to your victim.'

Rafferty leapt to his feet.

'Bejasus! One hundred dollars? Where in the name of St Patrick himself am I going to get one hundred dollars? I'd rather go to jail for a month.'

'Mr Rafferty,' the judge said solemnly, 'that is something I can instantly arrange.'

Reno sighed again. It was time to intervene.

Raising his hand to catch the attention of the judge, he got up from his seat. Heads turned and there were nods of recognition around the crowded room. Daniel Reno, former Civil War major — even though it was for the Rebs — was a highly respected businessman around Knoxville and when he spoke, people listened. Even inside the courtroom.

'Your Honour, maybe I can help solve this little problem.'

There was a murmur of interest from the crowd that brought the use of the gavel from the judge to restore order.

'I don't see that we have a problem, Mr Reno. Rafferty is condemned by words from his own mouth and I have decided that he will spend the next month in jail.'

'With respect, sir,' Reno had to check the rising sense of impatience, 'a month in jail for Mr Rafferty, though thoroughly deserved, will do little to compensate the unfortunate store owners as I believe you intended by the imposition of a fine.' He paused for effect and was happy to see the judge nod his agreement. 'Therefore, if I were to pay that one hundred dollars and take responsibility for Mr Rafferty's behaviour, perhaps that would satisfy all parties.'

'It would sure satisfy me, your lordship,' Rafferty shouted. The crowd laughed and even the judge raised a smile.

'I'm sure it would, Mr Rafferty, but then you would be walking out of this court a free man.'

Reno raised his hand again. 'No, Your Honour, I would expect Mr Rafferty to repay the money by working for me.'

The idea appealed to the judge, silenced the Irishman and satisfied Daniel Reno. He left the courtroom happy with the outcome. Rafferty was his man. All he had to wait for now was the arrival of Ethan Cole and his team would be complete.

★   ★   ★

Frank Mason suffered in silence for the rest of the journey while Ethan had the growing feeling that even Dutch and the fourth man, who he had discovered was the colourful Snake Delaney, had developed a grudging respect, no doubt springing from the result of the fist fight. Conversations were short and clipped but gone was the earlier hostility. Ethan had made a telling point but he knew that things could change just as quickly and Frank Mason was not the sort of man who would forgive and forget. Whatever Daniel Reno's plans, if they involved Mason, Ethan knew he would have to watch his back.

The sun was bright in the cloudless spring sky when Mason spoke for the first time since the fight. He raised his arm and signalled for the others to stop. He twisted painfully in his saddle, his voice little more than a hoarse whisper as he tried to speak through swollen lips.

'Over there. That's where the major will meet you.'

Ethan followed the direction indicated by Mason's pointing finger. Across the field was a small farmhouse isolated from a row of single-storey buildings that Ethan recognized as the outskirts of a small town.

Ethan was about to ask for details of the time of the meeting when Mason suddenly sat upright in his saddle and pulled on the reins.

'This ain't over between us, Cole. You won't have the major watching over you for the rest of your life.' Turning away, he signalled to the others to follow and the trio headed off in the direction of Knoxville a few miles along the river.

Ethan sat alone and studied the landscape he remembered from more than two years earlier; the small town of Concord and the Battle of Campbell's Station. It was on that day in November '63 that Reno had dragged him to safety as he stared death in the face. It was greener now with none of the stench of war to ruin the peace of a sunny afternoon; none of the sounds of gunfire, of cannons and the screams of dying soldiers from both sides that ripped a nation apart for four years and cost more than half a million lives.

And for what? Ethan reflected coldly. Families had been torn asunder and the distrust between North and South was unaffected by the signing of a treaty that stopped the killing but left the differences unresolved.

Now he was back at the scene of one of those bitter battles that had convinced him that the war was a futile waste of human life. Almost one thousand young men, including some 600 of Lt. General James Longstreet's southern troops had been killed or wounded in that battle on 16 November.

Ethan sat and watched the trio disappear into the distance before turning to complete the rest of the journey from Clarkston. He made his way slowly towards the farmhouse which he approached with some caution. The pain and scars from his brutal struggle with Frank Mason were still causing him severe problems. His ribs ached and his face bore the bruises and scratches of some ugly tactics.

Dismounting, he led his tired horse to a welcome trough, wrapped the reins around a handy hitching rail and hobbled up the three steps that led to the house. He was reaching out to enter when the door was suddenly jerked open and he found himself staring into the barrel of a shotgun.

'That's close enough, mister. What you want?'

'Hold it, lady,' Ethan said, backing away. 'I don't mean you any harm.'

The woman, a short, stockily built figure Ethan guessed to be in her fifties, wasn't convinced and held the rifle steadily, pointing it straight at her unwelcome visitor's chest.

'You look like trouble to me, stranger,' she said. 'You sure didn't get that face at a church social.'

Ethan tried to laugh but the pain in his ribs made that tricky.

'Like I said, what do you want?'

'Lady, could you point that thing somewhere else. It makes me nervous.'

'It stays until I get some answers. Now, who are you and what do you want will do for starters.'

Ethan visibly relaxed. She wasn't going to shoot him.

'I think you'll find I'm expected. The name's Ethan Cole.'

The woman lowered the rifle. 'Your name's Cole? In that case you'd better come inside. The major said you'd be coming by, except he didn't say you'd be alone. There were supposed to be four of you.'

Ethan grinned even though it hurt. 'There were four of us, we — er — we didn't get along too well.' He felt the bruises on his face and gently rubbed his injured ribs.

The woman stepped aside and let him into the house. 'If you're still standing I'd hate to see the state of the other fellas.'

She stood the rifle against a walnut cabinet and followed him into the room.

'My name's Sarah Tomkins. Maybe you heard the major mention me?' When Ethan said nothing, she went on: 'No matter. I've patched up worse than you — the major hisself for one. There's some hot coffee on the stove. Help yourself while I see what I can find to tend to your cuts and bruises.'

She left the room and Ethan took her advice, pouring himself a welcome hot drink and looking around the room for a comfortable chair to rest his aching limbs. It was a small room sparsely furnished. The best Ethan could find was a well-worn armchair next to an open, unlit fireside. A table, next to a side window, two wooden chairs and a stove and wash basin completed the furnishings.

Over to the right were two other doors which he guessed led to bedrooms.

He sipped the coffee, strong, hot and very welcome, and when Sarah Tomkins returned carrying a basin, towels and an armful of ointments, it was all he could do to keep his eyes open. It had been a long, hard ride from Clarkston and he badly needed his sleep before he challenged Daniel Reno.

He did not protest when the woman started to wipe away the dried blood from his facial wounds and to treat his bruises with a foul-smelling mixture from one of her bottles. But he groaned when she accidentally leaned too heavily on his ribs.

'Let's have that shirt off your back, mister. Strikes me those ribs could need some strapping.'

Again he didn't argue, gingerly pulling his shirt over his head and allowing his nurse to wrap the bandaging tightly around his bruised chest.

When she had finished her ministrations, she took the empty coffee cup from his grasp and said. 'I reckon the major won't be here much before sundown so I'd say you could do worse than get yourself some sleep.'

'Where is he, the major?' Ethan asked.

'He's in Knoxville, where do you think he is going to be? He's got his business to run.'

She turned away and went through the door that led, Ethan assumed, to the kitchen area.

So, Daniel Reno had a business to run. What sort of business? And why in a place like Knoxville? They were questions that could be answered later. Right now, Ethan was ready to take Sarah Tomkins' advice. He needed the sleep. Rising from his chair he wandered to the first door and pushed it open. It was, as he had guessed, a bedroom. But more than that. As he stood in the open doorway his jaw dropped. He was staring at a shrine. A shrine to the Confederate army.

Filling most of the far wall was a huge Confederate battle flag with its thirteen golden stars and alongside it, torn and fading, was the Confederates' first national flag, the Stars and Bars.

On a dressing table was a framed picture of the Confederacy's only president, Jefferson Davis. The room also contained an array of war memorabilia: pistols, a cannon ball, even a personal letter from Robert E. Lee after the surrender in '65.

But the figure that dominated the room was a tall, perfectly proportioned model dressed in the full grey uniform of a Confederate major. The face of the figure had been moulded to include a full grey moustache, a neatly trimmed beard and a battle scar on the left cheek. There was no mistake: the face was exactly as Ethan remembered Daniel Reno.

Backing out of the room, Ethan was caught unawares when he almost bumped in to Mrs Tomkins. She made no effort to move aside.

'You shouldn't have gone in there, Mr Cole. That's the major's private quarters. And you can see why I had to take precautions when you arrived at the house. It wouldn't do to let the wrong people into the house now, would it?'

Ethan rested his hand on the woman's shoulder. 'I can see that, Mrs Tomkins. But don't worry, the secret's safe with me. There is no need for the major to know I've been in the room.'

The woman relaxed. 'Thank you, sir. Now, if you still need that rest, the other room is ready. You won't be disturbed in there.'

She turned away and Ethan stood and watched her go. Who was she? And what was the reason for the memorial room? Daniel Reno had a lot of questions to answer when he arrived at the farmhouse. Ethan was still thinking about the room and Mrs Tomkins when he fell asleep.

★　★　★

The sound of raised voices broke into Ethan's troubled sleep. Straining to hear, he could make out that Frank Mason was quarrelling with an Irishman whose voice he did not recognize. The sounds were loud but indistinct and they were suddenly interrupted by the voice of authority. Major Daniel Reno was in control.

Ethan swung his legs over the side of the bed and sat upright. The voices from the other room became more controlled and the discussion, as far as he could tell, was less heated.

His ribs still ached and a glance in the bedroom mirror told him that the bruises were still ugly but the scratches had lost their fire. But, whatever his appearance, though, the time had come to face the major. He would learn why he had been brought to this isolated farmhouse under forced escort. And he would learn what Reno was planning. He strode across the bedroom floor and pulled open the door.

There were seven men in the room but it was Reno who stood in the centre, tall, erect and in full control. He had thickened around the waist since the last time Ethan had seen him. The Battle of Five Forks had been the final nail in the coffin of the Confederacy but Ethan remembered it only for the death of his brother.

As the door opened, Reno turned to face him. There was no friendly smile of greeting — the major had never been a man who took easily to smiling — but he had not expected one. Even so, he sensed that Reno was pleased to see him and the handshake was as firm as ever.

'Ethan, my boy! Welcome from your slumbers.' He stood back and examined the other's scarred and bruised face. 'I have been informed that your meeting with Frank was not as amicable as I had hoped. I have had words with him.' He sighed.

'No matter, that is all behind us all now.'

Ethan couldn't prevent a quiet smile. The letter that Frank Mason had delivered back in Clarkston had been a reminder of the major's love of high-sounding language and now, even as he surveyed the results of a vicious brawl between two of his trusted men, he had no inclination to curse or blaspheme.

He turned away and faced the others in the room.

'Gentlemen, this is Captain Ethan Cole, one of the finest horse riders and shooters ever to wear the Confederate uniform. Ethan will be my second in command during the campaign. If I become indisposed for any reason Captain Cole will be the officer giving the orders. Is that understood?'

There were grunts of reluctant agreement — Frank Mason remained silent — before the Irishman said with a challenge in his tone: 'A fine horseman are you, sir? Now, we'll have to test the major's judgement on that announcement for sure.'

Ethan eyed the red-haired figure in the tattered shirt and stained pants who moved forward to thrust out a podgy hand.

'The name's Rafferty, Captain. Martin Rafferty, late of Donegal, Ireland. Now there's a place where they know all about horse flesh.'

Ethan took the man's hand. 'I've heard it said, Mr Rafferty, that the Irish are, indeed, good judges of horses, especially the women.'

The jibe wasn't lost on the redhead but it was the friendly banter that was needed to break the ice that had developed from the moment Reno introduced him to the rest. He didn't know these men and they did not know him. But they did know more than he did — they all clearly knew why they were there.

Ethan released the Irishman's hand and turned to Reno.

'Daniel — ?'

'Major, Captain Cole. From now on it is Major Reno.'

Ethan took the reprimand with a smile.

'Major, you talked about a campaign as though, well, as though the war was still on. As though we were still fighting the North.'

Daniel Reno coughed and put his arm around Ethan's shoulder. 'Sorry, Captain. I must confess to a force of habit but, in one sense that is why we are all here. Why I needed you, my trusted comrades, by my side. Had things gone better in Clarkston then Sergeant Mason would have explained everything.'

He paused and then added: 'I did not put things into my letter for obvious reasons. If something had happened to Mason on his way to you who knows into whose hands the letter may have fallen.'

Ethan waited for further explanation and when it came it felt as though his whole peaceful world as a small town Tennessee storekeeper collapsed around him.

'This is a campaign in the true sense, Captain,' Reno said after a long silence. 'In two days' time this small band of soldiers will relieve the Washington government of almost half a million dollars worth of gold bullion. And we shall use it to re-arm and regenerate the Confederate cause. We are going to rob a train.'

4

This is madness!

That thought struck Ethan for the third time as he stood on the porch and studied the clouds passing across the moon. For the past hour he had listened mostly in a state of total silence bordering on disbelief to Daniel Reno outlining his master plan.

The major ordered the diverse group of gunmen and former soldiers into the room Ethan had stumbled into in error earlier. The life-sized uniformed model had been removed and seven hard-backed chairs had been placed around the wall. Reno stood in front of the picture of Jefferson Davis and ordered the others to take their seats.

'Two days from now a train of the East Tennessee and Georgia Railroad will be passing through Concord and Knoxville transporting up to half a million dollars' worth of gold bullion bound eventually for Washington. We will be relieving that train of its consignment.

'There are those who foolishly believed that the Confederacy died when Robert E. Lee signed that shameful document of surrender at Appottomax; that the South would meekly submit to the rule of Lincoln and his false promises.'

Reno paused and allowed himself a smug chuckle. 'Thankfully, he had only four days to gloat over his triumph before Wilkes Booth did the world a service. He deserves the gratitude of all southerners for what he achieved at that theatre.'

Ethan looked around the room to try to deduce the reaction of the others. But there was none. They were engrossed in the major's speech.

'Those who thought our struggle was lost, and I don't include any of my loyal comrades in this room, can now believe in our cause again. As I speak to you now thousands of men, many thousands in Texas alone, are ready to re-arm and renew the struggle for our rights.'

His voice was starting to rise. 'We are not common outlaws; we are not stealing this gold to increase our own wealth. It will be used to support the New Confederacy army. We may be only a small band but believe me there are many more willing to take up arms and shed their blood again. By striking this first blow for the people of the Southern States we will be writing the first page in a new chapter of this country's history. We have not come this far, spilled so much blood and lost so many loved ones to give up our just fight. You have been chosen because I know from past experience that you are the right men to revive the cause. If you have any doubts, now is the time to voice them.'

Ethan waited for somebody to speak. Nobody did. He studied Reno's face. Was this man disturbed? Did he really think that a four-year war that cost some 600,000 lives of men from both sides was not a big enough price to pay? That a few thousand disillusioned Texans and a handful of like-minded men of Tennessee could alter the course of history?

Ethan got to his feet.

'Major, this is the first I have heard about your plans and while I don't doubt your sincerity — '

'I hope not, Captain,' Reno interrupted with a rare smile. 'But, please, I am interested in your thoughts. As always.'

Ethan could see he was going to get no support from the others and that he would have to tread carefully. If Daniel Reno was as deranged as he had begun to sound, there was no telling what his reaction would be to any criticism, however mild.

'Sir, you have clearly not been idle since . . . since Lee's surrender,' he had to avoid the phrase 'since the war ended', 'and you are well respected for your intelligence gathering — '

'Get to the point, Captain!' Frank Mason barked. 'Or are you looking for a way to back out? If that's the case, then me and the boys will oblige you.'

Dutch and the others chuckled but Reno waited for Ethan to continue.

'How do you know the gold is on that train?'

Reno tapped the table. A nervous twitch, Ethan wondered.

'On that, you will simply have to trust me — and I am sure I can rely on that, Ethan.' He had dropped the formality. 'Before your arrival, I explained to the others that we have a special bond and that you would be as enthusiastic as I about this campaign. You are not going to tell me I am about to be disappointed?'

Ethan said nothing. Instead, he sat down and listened without really hearing the plans being outlined by the major.

Later, as he stood alone on the porch, the others having long since returned to wherever they were camped, he wondered how he could extricate himself from what he knew was an ambitious man's crazy scheme to restart a war.

'Rain's coming.' Ethan turned to see Mrs Tomkins standing in the doorway of the house. He studied the woman closely for the first time. She was a few years older than he first imagined, probably into her late fifties or early sixties.

Although it was only a vague feeling, he wondered where he had seen her face before. The thought passed as quickly as it arrived when she suddenly said: 'You appear to have something on your mind, Mr Cole. I've been watching you and I — er — ' She stammered, clearly uncertain whether she should continue.

Ethan waited; a silence she took to be encouragement.

'I have the feeling that you're not completely happy with what the major has planned. Am I right?'

It was Ethan's turn to pause before

answering. What could he say? He could hardly tell the woman the truth, that he was even starting to doubt the major's sanity. And even if Daniel Reno was still in control of his wits and competence, the chances of a successful raid on a bullion-carrying train with eight assorted strangers would be impossible. And even if it did succeed, how was the gold going to be distributed to fund his so-called resurgent army? Once again, thoughts of the major's madness crossed his mind.

'Your silence tells me all I need to know,' Sarah Tomkins said before Ethan could answer.

He smiled at her. 'Maybe I am the cautious type, Mrs Tomkins. Two days ago I was a storekeeper in Clarkston, a small remote town in Southern Tennessee. I was a retired soldier who had settled comfortably into peace time. I haven't used a rifle or a side gun since the war ended. Mason and his two sidekicks dragged me here but it was the major's letter that intrigued me. He knew I would come — he didn't need those three hirelings to persuade me.'

'He wasn't sure any more,' she answered thoughtfully. 'Time has passed. People change.'

'But Daniel Reno hasn't changed,' Ethan interrupted her. 'He seriously believes that he can spark another Southern armed rebellion.'

She nodded. 'But Daniel isn't alone. Throughout Tennessee and down in Texas and Alabama and Mississippi there are growing signs that people still believe Washington to be the enemy. These men are looking for a man to lead them — somebody with the backbone to show the North that they cannot ride roughshod over the South.'

Like Reno earlier, her voice was rising to a passion that disturbed and worried Ethan.

'And Reno thinks he is that man?' he mused aloud. 'What is your feeling, Mrs Tomkins. Why are you here?'

She shuffled awkwardly. 'This is my

home. The war cost me a husband and a son, Mr Cole. I have no love for the North so when Daniel came to me and told me what he was planning to do and asked if he could use my little farmhouse as his campaign headquarters I was happy to agree. Now . . . ' Ethan sensed there was more to come, 'I am not so sure. Oh, it's not that I doubt Daniel or his sincerity but I believe that some of his men, and others, are not the loyal soldiers he believes them to be.

'Mr Cole,' another pause, 'I hope I can trust you. Daniel has always spoken highly of his captain. How the best thing he did throughout the war was to save your life.'

There it was again, the reminder of what Ethan actually owed Daniel Reno. But there was something else behind Sarah Tomkins' gushing flow of trust in a man she had met only a few hours earlier. She spotted the quizzical look in his eye.

'I see you are wondering why I am

telling you all this but it's simple really,' she explained.

Her explanation was indeed simple, and it also clarified an earlier puzzle about where he had seen her face before.

'I fear for Daniel's life. He's my brother.'

5

The rains that Sarah Tomkins had warned were threatening arrived well into the night but Ethan was already fully awake. He had had no sleep since turning in shortly after midnight. Instead he had stared up at the roof of the back room in the farmhouse, his mind totally occupied with thoughts of what lay ahead over the next two days.

Twice during the night he was tempted to sneak out of the house and ride away from this approaching nightmare but each time he dismissed the idea. Running out would achieve nothing. Reno and his crew of hired gun hands would go through with the raid on the train in the belief that they were fighting and funding a revived Southern cause and when it was over they would hunt him down. And next time Daniel Reno would claim what he believed he was owed: Ethan Cole's life. But the deeper he thought about the major's plan, the more Ethan realized that, whatever his misgivings, he would have to wait for his chance to foil the robbery and in doing so save Reno from his own folly.

He knew that the major was not the only disillusioned Confederate officer unable to come to terms with life after the war; it was more than likely that Sarah Tomkins was right when she spoke of pockets of ex-militia men throughout the Southern states. And if that was the case, Ethan knew from his own experience that Reno would see himself as the leader of the New Confederacy. If he needed more proof it came in the bedroom shrine that included that life-sized model of Reno himself in full uniform.

The rain had stopped by daybreak and the sky was almost cloudless when the sun rose above the eastern mountains. But the bright morning brought

Ethan no closer to a solution to his problem. He was halfway through his second cup of coffee when he was joined by Daniel Reno. Ethan rose from his seat at the kitchen table but Reno offered one of his rare smiles.

'Stay seated, Captain, you look tired. It has been a traumatic two days for you. I understand that, my friend. But when the time comes you will be fine.'

He patted Ethan on the shoulder, like a favourite uncle comforting an errant nephew, and walked across the room to where his sister was cooking a breakfast. He poured himself a coffee and returned to the table, taking a chair opposite Ethan.

'I trust you had a comfortable night,' Reno said eager to continue the one-sided conversation. Ethan eyed him closely. As ever, the man was immaculately groomed and spoke as articulately and convincingly as he remembered. Whatever his current mindset, Ethan tried to believe that Daniel Reno was still a true gentleman.

But he didn't speak. This was the time to listen. There was no Frank Mason, no Dutch or Snake, no others to listen and nod and agree to his every word. This was between Daniel Reno and the man whose life he had saved. His only friend.

It did not take Reno long to get to the point of this early morning meeting. And Ethan was happy to be given the chance to speak when the time came.

'I have to say something, my friend, and I trust you will not be offended. You disappointed me yesterday. I can accept that men like Mason and the others do not have the wit or wisdom to see beyond their limited brains but I had hoped that you would not be the one to question my strategy.'

Ethan gestured as if to speak but Reno held up his hand to prevent any interruption. 'Was I being too optimistic when I hoped that you would come as soon as you read the letter, after all we went through together?'

'Is that why you sent Mason and his

two personal skunks along?' Ethan said not trying to hide the hint of sarcasm. 'Yes, I was intrigued enough to come along and now that I am here I am not sure why.'

Suddenly, Daniel Reno stood up and marched, military-style across the room. Turning, he almost barked the next question. 'Did you know, Ethan, that our president is still in prison? After all he has done for all Americans Jefferson Davis is being treated like a common criminal. A more upright and moral man you would never meet, but he is being held for treason. Is this the sort of benevolence and fair-mindedness that Lincoln promised when Lee signed that damned paper a year ago?

'Lincoln may be long dead and gone and I don't want to malign the man but his legacy lives on in that vain tailor Andrew Johnson who is now in the White House. He is openly hostile to the South. And he, a man from the Carolinas.'

The major was in full flow but Ethan was hardly listening. How could he take seriously anything this man was saying? He was becoming insanely deluded.

The idea of robbing a train to help finance a second attempt to form a Confederacy; or the belief that throughout the South like-minded men were banding together into armed military detachments were, Ethan thought, pure fantasy.

His thoughts were interrupted when Reno unexpectedly said: 'I need you here, Captain and I apologize if my methods were, shall we say, clumsy. Mason and the others are simply hired guns. I am not even certain that they believe in this campaign.'

Ethan remained silent as he tried to picture the events of the next two days. It would not be the first time he had broken the law — nor even the first time he had robbed a train, but was he still the man who in his youth had flouted authority and, if he cared to admit to himself, had joined the

Southern army as much for the thrills and adventure as a share in the ideology of men like Daniel Reno?

'I can see you also have your doubts, my friend,' the major continued. 'That is understandable. After all, you have settled into the quiet life of a small town storekeeper who is caring for his brother's widow and her young son,' his raised hand prevented any interruption, 'and if the reports I received are to be believed, you are pursuing a romantic interest in the lady.'

Ethan stiffened and Reno made a point of noticing the reaction.

'You look surprised that I should know these things, Captain. Didn't I tell you that my intelligence gathering was widespread? But you need not concern yourself. I like to keep a trace on the men who served with me and I can assure you nothing will happen to the delightful Mrs Cole or the young boy, Jonathan.'

Ethan said nothing but there was menace in Daniel Reno's words. This was a clear threat and a signal that a long-standing friendship was reaching its end.

'Of course, I need something from you to assure you of your family's continued well-being.'

Again Ethan waited.

'Yes, indeed,' Reno said with an exaggerated sigh. 'I can see that the year of inactivity has softened you considerably and I cannot permit that. I need the Captain Ethan Cole who was at my side when the bullets were flying and the cannons discharging here at Knox County or Five Forks. I do not need a small town storekeeper worrying about some woman and her boy.'

Ethan decided that it was time to speak. Further silence would be a sign of weakness, surrender, even. Rising from his seat he stood toe to toe with the man with revolution still burning inside him. Neither flinched as they faced each other in the centre of the room.

'Are you threatening me, major? Is

this your idea of inspiring loyalty in a friend? A man whose life you claim to have saved?'

'I think it is better this way, Captain. We have a very important campaign ahead of us — '

'Campaign!' Ethan spat out the word. 'This is nothing more than a train robbery. There is no secret army building up for a new fight for Southern freedom. No upsurge in the Confederate cause. The war is over. Lost. Gone. In God's name, Daniel, why can't you accept that?'

Daniel Reno turned away but there was no anger in his voice when he spoke. He was calm, controlled.

'It is a pity you feel that way, my friend, but no matter. We can live with your misplaced loyalties until the time comes for you to meet the men who will convince you that the resurgence is real. As for your assumption that I am issuing some sort of threat, I am merely explaining the protection I have taken should you decide to make any attempt to impede the aims of myself and those loyal to the South.'

'A fancy speech, Daniel,' Ethan snapped. 'But you were always good with words. Well, here is something for you to think about. I will be your captain. I will go along with your crazy scheme, but as soon as it is over I am heading to my home. If anything should happen to Alice or her son, believe me, I will come after you. Yesterday, I promised to kill Frank Mason if he so much as crossed my path again. Now I am saying the same thing to you. Harm my family in any way and, as God is my judge, I will kill you.'

Snatching his hat from the table, he stormed out of the house, strode across the yard to the corral where he had left his horse, mounted up and headed at a gallop across the pastureland that bordered the Tennessee River. He had to put as much distance as he could between himself and Daniel Reno.

Behind him, his face set in grim

satisfaction, the major stood on the porch of the farmhouse and watched him go. Ethan Cole was good and mad and that was the way he wanted him to be.

He turned to the woman who had stepped out of the house.

'As long as he thinks his brother's widow and his nephew are in danger, his mind will concentrate on everything I tell him, Sarah.'

Sarah Tomkins nodded but she was not convinced. Was her brother seriously mad? There was fire in his eyes and it was a fire she had hoped that Ethan Cole could control. Now she was not so sure.

As the pair went back into the house, Daniel was sure of one thing: by the time Ethan Cole learned the real reason behind his presence it would be far too late; America would be plunged into another civil war and this time there would be no surrender by either side.

★　★　★

Ethan dismounted and tied his horse reins to a nearby bush before strolling down to the river's edge. Crouching, he swilled his face with the ice-cold water. It helped to clear his head but he felt no better for the experience.

Daniel Reno was truly out of control. The idea that thousands of Southern men were gathering together to spill more blood for a lost cause that had already cost so many lives, was in itself crazy. But Daniel believed it and, even more implausibly, he also believed that he was the man to lead this new insurrection.

As he gazed out at the distant mountain range and watched the sun's rays dancing on the flowing waters of the river, Ethan found himself reminded of his Bible classes, of Moses leading the Israelites to the Promised Land. Did Captain Reno believe he was another Moses? Or maybe a different biblical character altogether. He reflected on Daniel in the Lion's Den.

He did not know how long or how far

he had ridden but he knew that he would have to return to the farmhouse eventually. He had told Reno that he would be part of his train robbery plan and he also knew that, if he failed to return, Alice and Jonathan would be in danger. Daniel Reno did not issue threats he had no intention of following through.

The peaceful occupation of a Clarkston storekeeper seemed like another lifetime. Ethan lost all sense of time as he sat at the water's edge and allowed his thoughts to drift back to that November day more than two years earlier.

* * *

Like most of his men, Ethan had known that the Civil War was going badly, that despite Lee's efforts and urgings, heavy defeats were taking their toll.

Daniel Reno was not among the men willing to concede that the North were gaining ground day by day. Even as the battle raged and men in grey fell dying around him, the major fought to defy the overwhelming odds.

Things were going badly as the federal forces pushed back the lines and the Confederate troops were compelled to make a hurried and disorganized retreat. It was during the chaos of falling bodies and the flashes of gunfire that Ethan Cole found himself staring death in the face.

The figure in the torn, bloodstained blue jacket emerged through the fog of gunsmoke. Ethan raised his handgun and squeezed the trigger.

Nothing. He tried again. The same result.

The trooper closed in, a hint of madness in his staring blue eyes. Ethan steeled himself. The man had a rifle, one of those new, rapid loading Springfields. Why didn't he shoot? Why did he keep advancing? Less than two feet separated them when the reality struck Ethan: the man had been blinded. His wild, staring blue eyes were sightless.

Stumbling forward, he collided heavily with Ethan and the pair crashed to the ground. Together they tumbled into a trench and the blinded man let out a scream of agony when he rolled into a jagged rock and the impact sent a searing pain through his already badly damaged left leg.

Ethan regained his feet and started to scramble out of the ditch. He couldn't fight a blind man, a man who was so badly wounded that he could be dead long before the day was over.

Peering through the thickening smoke, Ethan managed to make out the shadowy figures of men in hand to hand combat and whinnying horses, shying away in terror at the deafening sound of gunshots. As he reached the top of his climb Ethan found himself in a state of total confusion. All around him men were dying; others running aimlessly in search of refuge from the battle.

Then, out to his left, came a voice he knew so well.

'Captain! Over here, man!'

The smoke may have disguised the identity of the caller but there was no mistaking the refined tones. Rushing in the direction of Daniel Reno's voice, Ethan caught sight of the major in the sort of pose he always frivolously assumed the man spent hours practising, swishing his sabre above his head and barking orders.

But that must have been a trick played on him by his imagination. This was the heat of battle and the Daniel Reno who emerged into view wasn't playing games. Urging his horse forward, he reached down and hauled Ethan up behind him.

'All is lost here, Captain! We must make good our escape. We must live to fight another day. We will stay together and will have better days!'

Ethan remembered little else. The major's horse had galloped less than a hundred yards when their escape route was suddenly blocked by exploding cannon fire. The horse reared up and threw both men to the ground. Blackness engulfed him when his head hit the hard ground with a sickening thud.

★ ★ ★

By mid-afternoon, Frank Mason and the others were back at the farmhouse. But there was still no sign of Ethan Cole.

'He will be here,' Reno insisted, snubbing Mason's suggestion that the captain had run out on them.

Mason was not alone in believing that Ethan had deserted the group. The Irishman Rafferty was of the same opinion while the rest simply believed what they saw with their own eyes. The captain was nowhere to be seen which told them all they needed to know.

None of them was blessed with the patience needed when there was time to kill and, although he refused to admit as much, Reno was angry with Cole.

He would demand an explanation for his absence when he eventually returned — which, of course he would — and he would need a reminder of the consequences should he ever consider desertion.

The frustrating wait led to an uneasy silence among the group, broken only by a mean or nasty reference to the missing man.

Reno sensed the growing tension but he knew that, without Cole, there was little point in outlining his final plans. This was to be an eight-man operation and it was Cole and Mason who would be boarding the train at the start of its journey. They would be the two who would order the engineer to make his unscheduled stop at the cutting near the border of Knox County. No campaign could be successful without sacrifice. Mason was nothing more than a hired gun and was expendable although it was a pity about Ethan Cole. But what were their lives compared to the ultimate prize that Reno had in his sights.

He was still thinking about this when Rafferty, who had spent almost an hour staring out of the window, suddenly rose from his seat.

'There's a rider coming and to my way of thinking it looks like our missing Mr Cole.'

6

Daniel Reno folded his map carefully and slid it back into the drawer of the table. He had told this group all they needed to know.

'That is it, gentlemen, you now have all your instructions. If there is anything you do not understand, or wish to know more, now is the time to speak. Tomorrow when we go our separate ways will be too late.'

There was a brief silence before Frank Mason got to his feet.

'There's one thing, major. Why me and Cole?' He glanced across at Ethan who had been wondering the same but decided that silence was the wisest option. He knew from experience that once Reno had made a decision there would be no going back. He had his reasons for pairing up the two men who had most reasons to hate each other.

'I was wondering if you would ask that question, Sergeant. You didn't disappoint me.'

Mason scowled. 'So? Tell us.'

'I believe you are the best men for this role. You have shown me personal loyalty, Frank and I trust the captain implicitly. I have another reason too.' He offered a weak excuse for a smile. 'I know you won't shoot each other, at least until our mission is completed. After that . . . '

It was the Irishman who laughed loudest. 'How about the rest of us, major? How are we to know that somebody isn't going to put a bullet in our back? How about you, Dutch? I reckon your lot don't think too much of the Irish.'

Reno picked up his hat. The meeting was over.

'From this moment we are on a military footing. I suggest we all get a good night's sleep. By this time tomorrow we will have enough gold to finance a new armed force strong enough to send a signal to Washington that the South will not be ruled from some distant White House but from a rebuilt Richmond. And we will start that message by freeing our president, Jefferson Davis.

★ ★ ★

Frank Mason dismounted outside the small hotel. The town was quiet at that late hour, the only signs of life coming from the saloon at the far end of the street. Slowly tying his horse's reins to the hitching rail, Mason studied the deserted street. He had to be careful even though he was convinced that Reno suspected nothing. The old fool was far too obsessed with his crazy dream of leading the South into another useless war. Mason was convinced that all his high-minded talk of Texans rebelling, of Tennessee and Alabama regrouping their forces, of his own standing among the diehard Southerners as a possible leader, were the ravings of a mad man. And a madman who believed he was indestructible; so the idea that he may be betrayed never entered his head.

Mason rubbed his stubbled chin. The swelling of his jaw had subsided but the pain was a reminder that he still had a score to settle. But he did agree with one point Reno had made: he would keep his revenge on Cole until this raid was over.

Satisfied that he was not being watched, Mason mounted the three steps and entered the hotel. Across the room he immediately spotted the man he had come to see — a tall, slim figure in a long black coat. The man's long, pointed features, grey locks and deep set dark eyes suggested he was in his fifties but Jackson Blake had not yet reached forty years of age.

As with so many men, the war had taken a heavy toll on his life and as he walked across the room to greet Mason he leaned heavily on a black, pearl-handled stick.

His face broke into a welcoming smile as the pair shook hands.

'I trust you have some good news for me, Frank,' the man said, his voice unusually high pitched.

'As we expected. The raid will go ahead tomorrow as planned.'

'Good. Then I will have our men in place. We leave our arrogant Major Reno to allow his vanity to rule his reason and allow him to carry out his plan. And then, my friend, we will step in and reap the rewards.'

Mason nodded. Blake knew what he was doing, unlike that power-crazed fool and self-styled major, Reno.

Frank Mason shuffled uncomfortably. Jackson Blake was one of the few men who made him feel uneasy. Nobody had ever succeeded in doing that but Blake was different. Maybe it was those deep set eyes, the weather-beaten features or the cold toneless voice, Mason couldn't figure it out. But he couldn't trust the man; he wasn't somebody Frank would turn his back on.

'I want Ethan Cole,' Mason snarled. He rubbed the bruising on his face — a reminder of the brutal fight they had on the road from Clarkston.

Blake nodded. 'We all have our demons, Frank. I have my own to drive out. All I want is that you carry out what we have planned. It will make you a very rich man and you can then fight your own private war.'

He watched Mason leave the hotel and then went back to his seat in the corner of the room and resumed reading his newspaper.

He knew that Mason sold his services to the highest bidder and he had paid well for the information on Reno's plans. Why employ a small army to raid a train when he could rely on somebody else to do the job for him? It would be far easier for him and his men to relieve Reno of his spoils than to attack what would be a heavily guarded train.

The thought amused him and he ordered another whiskey before entering the gaming room to join a lucrative

card game and pick out a woman for
the night.

★　★　★

Daniel Reno made his way slowly up
the embankment running alongside
the rail track and pointed his spyglass
towards the small, wooden shack. He
checked that all was in order; his
men were in their places. He lowered
his glass and dismounted. Reno was
back in his own private world; the
world that existed before that futile
war; the world where he did not
require a uniform to command
respect and obedience. One word was
enough.

It had long been that way at
Dudbridge; his spacious plantation
home deep in the South. Life had been
wonderful for himself and his sister
Sarah. They had ridden together,
hunted together and swam together.
Only when that pompous oaf Raymond
Tomkins appeared on the scene and

started to call on Sarah did they drift apart.

Tomkins, a small figure of a man — small in stature, small in mind to Daniel's way of thinking — starting calling following a chance meeting.

The Reno family were on one of their regular visits into the city. Sarah, well into her twenties but still unattached and uncourted, and Daniel, little more than a boy and eight years his sister's junior, were left to amuse themselves.

They wandered around the stores while their father conducted his plantation business and their mother visited other family members.

Daniel was examining some riding boots when he noticed the slight, sandy-haired figure looking at them through the doorway. It was clearly Sarah, though, who had caught the stranger's attention and by the time the day was over, the man had engineered his way to an introduction to the Reno family in general but to Sarah in particular.

Their courtship brought an end to the sister-brother partnership and, despite Daniel's best efforts to destroy the romance by his constant sniping at Tomkins' Northern background, the wedding went ahead as scheduled.

As he surveyed the scene below, Reno clearly remembered the conversation he had with his sister two days before the marriage ceremony conducted in the chapel at the Dudbridge plantation.

He had just completed a ride along one of the favourite stretches of land that he and Sarah had galloped before the arrival of Tomkins and was walking his horse along the edge of a remote river bank when she suddenly appeared out of a nearby woodland.

There was some uncomfortable small talk before Sarah eventually broke the news she had ridden out to deliver.

Daniel couldn't fail to notice that there was little sisterly love in her voice as she told him: 'Raymond and I will be leaving Dudbridge after the wedding ceremony, Daniel.'

'Leaving? To go where?'

'We will be going out East to live. To New York.'

There was an uncomfortable silence before Daniel eventually huffed his protest. 'New York? Sarah, you belong here . . . Dudbridge is your home. You were born here, like me. You can't leave!'

Then, for the first time in their lives, Sarah lectured her 16-year-old brother.

'My life has changed, Daniel. Soon I will be Mrs Raymond Tomkins and I have a duty to go where my husband says. You know he has business in the East and besides . . . ' her voice tailed off as she struggled to find the words that would explain another of the reasons behind the decision. Eventually it came in a burst.

'Raymond has already explained it to Father; he abhors the practice of slavery. He feels it is against God's will for one man to own another human being and everywhere he turns on the plantation he finds this is the case: blacks labouring in the cotton fields; their men folk ploughing from dawn till night time, the children — '

She turned away as she saw the look of fury in her brother's eyes.

'God's will? What the hell does a pompous puritan like Tomkins know about God's will? He comes here from his Northern industrial rich land, courts my sister and drags her off to the big city but not before telling us how to run our lives; how to conduct ourselves. What does he know about our slaves and how we treat them, the self-righteous bluenose.'

Sarah could see that there was no reasoning with her brother in this mood and she turned her horse to head back to the house. But Daniel grabbed at the reins and prevented her from riding off.

'Sarah, please.' His tone was conciliatory but his message was clear. 'I would like to wish you well, sister, but I cannot. Raymond Tomkins will not make you happy. He is not good enough for you.'

He turned away. 'Forgive me, Sarah, but I would rather not attend your wedding. I cannot sit and listen to a preacher calling on God and all present to witness what I know to be wrong.'

Sarah said nothing. It was the last he saw of her until their father's funeral some ten years later.

* * *

Lucas Reno had lived all but the first five of his years in the Carolinas so life on a plantation was in his blood. Dudbridge had been his home for as long as he could remember, passing on from his own father to himself and his brother Jacob — a man with a roving eye and a roving mind who could never settle to domesticity and was never heard of again once Lucas had wished him a fond farewell as he went in search of soldiering adventures with a sizeable donation in his purse.

Dudbridge had long been a prestigious and profitable estate built on the values of the South and Lucas had been a benevolent slave owner. It came as a shock to Daniel when his father suddenly called him into his private room to make his announcement.

Lucas Reno was not alone. His companion was a slim, straight-backed man whom Daniel had seen making several visits to Dudbridge during his youth, though, as far as he could recollect, the man had not called at the house for several years.

'Ah, Daniel,' his father said with a hint of pride as he entered the room. 'I don't think you have ever been introduced. 'He visibly expanded his ample chest and his voice almost cracked with the words. 'Daniel, I would like you to meet, Mr James Polk, the President of the United States.'

Daniel was shocked. He had heard his father speak of Polk, telling of the days they had studied law together in Nashville. How they had become very close friends. Indeed it had been Polk who had introduced Reno to the woman who was to become his wife (Daniel's mother) and he had often spoken proudly of his friendship of the man from North Carolina who had become the Governor of Tennessee. Since Polk's election as President his father had spoken very little of his old friend.

'Don't look so surprised, son,' his father chuckled. 'The President won't bite you, my boy.'

Polk also smiled. 'Indeed, I won't, Daniel. I had plenty of opportunity to do that when you were only a boy but I resisted. And how are you this day?'

Daniel shuffled uncomfortably. 'Fine, Mr President, thank you for asking.'

The awkward silence that followed was broken by another chuckle from Daniel's father. He was not known for his sense of humour but he appeared to be enjoying this moment.

'The president has come to ask for my help and advice and I am pleased to say that I have happily agreed.'

'Father?' Daniel was puzzled. What could the most powerful man in the country want from his father? His curiosity was soon satisfied.

'Sit down, Daniel,' his father ordered. 'We have something to say to you which I hope you will find to all our advantages.'

It was at that moment, just three days before his twenty-sixth birthday, that Daniel Reno became a slave owner, a man of some substance in the Carolinas and a future officer in the Confederate army.

Gradually the reason for the president's visit to Dudbridge to seek the help of an old friend was explained.

Daniel listened with growing interest and enthusiasm. In April of '46, just a few months earlier, a Mexican cavalry detachment of some 2,000 men had routed a US patrol, killing more than a dozen men north of the Rio Grande. It was this massacre that prompted President Polk and his Congress to declare war in May.

'Mexico had crossed the US boundary and spilled American blood on American soil,' Polk said, vehemently repeating his strong message to Congress that led to the declaration of war.

The president explained how he had sent a representative to Mexico City for talks over the purchase of disputed lands of the Rio Grande but the envoy returned without agreement and the Mexican people were openly hostile to the United States, so much so that they deposed their president. But Polk also knew that the war with Mexico was not universally popular, being called unjust and unholy in some quarters. And he would eventually need a statesman of some distinction to find a solution.

'Which is why I have come to speak with your father, Daniel,' he concluded.

Lucas Reno put his arm around his son's shoulder.

'It means, my boy, that I will have to leave Dudbridge in your capable care until I return.'

Except the old man never returned. Barely two weeks after he took up President Polk's commission he was killed in an otherwise unrecorded skirmish.

Lucas Reno's death changed the course of Daniel's life.

In the weeks that followed his father's death, Daniel hid himself away, drank heavily and rejected any offer of support, especially from his sister Sarah and her husband Raymond Tomkins who travelled from their New York home to attend the funeral.

When he eventually emerged from his self-imposed retreat, Daniel was a man full of hate, not only for the Mexicans who had killed his father but primarily for the men who had involved Lucas Reno in what Daniel believed was a greedy, land-grabbing war. Top of his list was President James Polk but his venom was aimed at the entire US Government in Washington.

A man full of hate became a tyrannical slave holder and it was the workers of Dudbridge who suffered as the years wore on. Daniel drove hard, lost what friends he had and his reputation among the cotton producers plummeted.

But he cared little about popularity and when the war came he was among the first to join the Confederate cause of Jefferson Davis. His loathing of the North had not diminished over the years and even when the war was lost, Reno refused to surrender. He celebrated the assassination of Abraham Lincoln by the actor Wilkes Booth by drinking himself into a stupor and flogging anybody unfortunate enough to be within reaching distance of him as he went on a rampage of uncontrollable aggression.

Dudbridge, abandoned by its owner, had rapidly become a dilapidated ruin and the desertion by the slaves left the estate manned only by loyal farm-hands during the years of the conflict. Even the return of his widowed sister had failed to cheer him. The news that

Raymond Tomkins had died, not fighting for his beloved North but of a fever, brought him little satisfaction.

Even Sarah refused to stay. She took her share of what remained of the Dudbridge riches and bought herself the small Tennessee farmhouse that was now his campaign headquarters.

Time had not healed the wounds or the bitterness but Daniel had grown to control his excesses. Now, as he surveyed the scene below, he knew that the time had come for him and his kind to rise up again and restore the old order.

Satisfied that his orders were being obeyed he remounted and headed back towards the house. In the next few hours he would strike another crushing blow for the cause. His contempt for Mason and the others knew no bounds although he was aware that Ethan Cole was unlike the rest. Their only interest in this campaign was to get their hands on the gold consignment that he had used to persuade them. Cleverly, he had embellished tales of an uprising in Texas to encourage them and then used the Irishman Rafferty to cajole the others. Everything was now in place. Very soon the name of Daniel Reno would be known across the states both north and south.

★　★　★

The strained silence between the two riders was broken when they pulled their horses to a halt outside the rail depot. Ethan could not understand why Daniel had teamed himself and Mason together — their mutual hostility was no secret — but he knew they had a task to perform and despite his growing unease that his former army major was becoming obsessed by an idiotic assumption that the Southern states were ready for further conflict he was determined to see it through. The sooner he could end his association with Daniel Reno, Mason and the others the quicker he could return to his life as a storekeeper. That was where his future lay. A life with young Jonathan and his mother . . . Mason had been right about that.

Leaning forward on the horn of his saddle, Ethan studied the scene some two hundred yards away to the right. The depot was a hive of activity as railway staff busied themselves loading crates and baggage aboard, while the fireman and engineer stocked up with fuel. But it was not the sight of the workers that held Ethan's interest and attention. The train, just four carriages long and standing idly at the depot ahead of its journey, was flanked by a line of blue-suited soldiers armed with rifles and clearly under orders to protect the valuable cargo.

'The major's gonna need more men than he reckoned if he thinks this is gonna be easy,' Mason said. 'Those blue jackets look as though they mean business.'

Ethan considered Mason's view of the situation. He had no idea of how much gold was supposed to be aboard the Nashville-bound train but it was clear that the cargo was valuable enough to warrant the security of more than a dozen troopers eager for the action denied them since the end of the war.

'That's Reno's worry, not ours,' Ethan replied. 'All we have to do is get aboard that train and make sure it stops where it is supposed to and the gold is where it should be. Then the mad Irishman and the others can do the rest.' He nudged his horse into action: 'Let's go.'

As the two men approached the livery stable where they planned to leave their horses, Ethan caught sight of a group of smartly-dressed business-men in deep discussion. They were huddled near the ticket office and appeared to be animated as if eager for the train to be on its way, which suited Ethan perfectly as he was just as motivated to have this job done.

Their horses duly stabled, Ethan and

Mason headed for the ticket office, elbowing their way through the crowd. But before they reached their destination, they were blocked by two grim-faced soldiers armed with rifles held firmly across their chests.

The one wearing sergeant stripes glowered at the pair.

'You men wanting on the train?' he asked, his voice having the sharp aggressive pitch of a man on the look-out for trouble and not too concerned how he found it.

'That's why we're here,' said Ethan, stepping in before Frank had the chance to have his say. 'We're going through to Nashville.'

'Then you leave them behind,' the soldier said, waving his rifle in the direction of the men's guns. 'No side arms allowed. You can pick them up when you get where you're heading. Meantime, hand them in to my man here. He'll take good care of them.'

Ethan sensed that Frank Mason was ready to challenge the sergeant and the last thing he needed was to draw attention to themselves.

Unbuckling his belt, Ethan tried to make light of the demand to surrender his six-gun. 'You look like you're expecting trouble, Sergeant. What's happening here?'

But the soldier wouldn't be drawn. 'Just hand in your guns, mister, get your tickets and get aboard. Makes no difference to me. I've got my orders.'

The soldier turned away and left his young corporal to collect the guns, which he then carried into the depot office.

'So you reckon you're gonna use your charm to talk our way to the gold, Cole?' Mason said, his voice heavy with sarcasm as they strolled towards the train.

Ethan chuckled. 'Right now, Frank — that's about all we've got. Come on, let's get on board and try to figure out how we get this train to stop where Reno wants it to stop.'

Ethan led the way into the third of

the four carriages and the two took up a vacant seat near the rear. Already in place at the door adjoining the two leading carriages were a couple of blue-suited armed guards.

'Well now we know where the gold is stored,' Ethan whispered. 'Now all we got to do is get past those guards to the engineer and persuade him it's in his best interests to do as we tell him.'

Again Mason was heavy on the scorn: 'And we do all this while our guns are locked up in some trunk guarded by a coupla blue coats. Listen, Cole, I reckon we ought to get out of here, pick up our horses and head back to Knoxville. Leastways we can tell the major what's going on here.'

But Ethan wasn't listening. His attention was drawn to the group of grey-suited businessmen who had been standing together outside the ticket office when they arrived at the depot. There were six of them but one, slightly shorter than the others, remained surrounded by his companions who occasionally glanced over their shoulders as though anxious that they were being watched or followed.

The man in the middle of the group was ushered aboard to be quickly followed by the rest of the party.

Mason, who had also been watching the men's arrival, offered a twisted grin.

'Reckon those guys don't want to let their gold out of their sight. Seems even they don't trust the US army.'

Ethan eyed up his fellow passengers. The carriage was almost full which could be an advantage when the time came for action. None of them looked likely to be offering any resistance. Across the passageway to his left a young couple had eyes only for each other — newly-weds if Ethan wasn't mistaken — while ahead of them two old ladies exchanged gossip with an enthusiasm he remembered from the days when his own grandmother kept the family up to date on all the comings and goings around town.

He had been too young to remember

much of what she had to say but her stories about almost everybody from the minister to the latest saloon girl had made his father chuckle and that was good enough for Ethan.

The rest of the carriage was occupied by passengers who appeared to be travelling alone. A fat man in a checked suit was clearly an under-pressure sales representative and there was a woman who reminded him vaguely of his own mother while up front a man dressed in black had his nose deep in the Good Book.

If there were to be any trouble it would come from the cowboy sitting opposite the clergyman. But he had already pulled his hat over his face and was settling down to enjoy a nap.

The rest of the passengers were a mixed bunch but none of them looked likely to make a stand. Like him, they would be unarmed.

But then, of course, there were the stone-faced guards who stood, feet apart, rifles hugged across their chests.

Ethan rose from his seat and walked forward. Instantly the two soldiers were on the alert but Ethan did not falter in his stride.

'Where you think you're headed, mister?'

It was the taller of the two men who took one step forward and spoke.

Ethan smiled pleasantly.

'Nowhere, I guess. Just wanted some air.'

'Not this way,' the man said.

Ethan shrugged and smiled again: 'What you got in there, soldier? Apart from our guns I mean?'

'None o' your business, mister. Now I suggest you go back to your seat and sit out this train ride. And if you still want some air, I suggest you head out back.'

Ethan touched his hat in mock salute and headed back to where he had left Frank Mason gazing out as the train started to gather speed.

'So, what do you know now that you didn't know before you started to sweet talk the soldier boy?'

Mason was clearly unimpressed by Ethan's attempt to find out more about the train's valuable cargo and when no answer came he added: 'We need to get to our guns. How are we gonna stop this train without guns?'

But Ethan ignored the question. He had other thoughts running through his mind. Instead he said 'How did Daniel get to know about the gold on this train, Frank?'

Mason sniggered. 'You know the major, Cole. He don't exactly open up to people like me. As far as I can figure it, he must have his spies out, specially if what he says about there being others out there keen to get the South back into action.'

'Spies.' Ethan repeated the word quietly. 'Yeah, that would be my guess, too. D'you know, Frank, I think we should just settle down and enjoy the trip. I have a feeling that something might happen before we get close to Knoxville. Meantime, we just wait.'

'Wait? Wait for what?'

Ethan wasn't sure, but if he was guessing right then the surrender of their guns was not the handicap it was intended to be.

Experience told him that Daniel Reno was not the trusting sort. He had paired him and Frank Mason for a reason. Maybe it was because he didn't trust Frank. Or he didn't trust Ethan. Or both. Which meant that whoever had been Daniel's informant about the gold, his spy, could well be aboard this train. And if that was the case then he was sure to show himself before the train neared the cutting that was to be the scene of the raid. Only time would tell.

The train sped on its journey without incident and Ethan began to wonder if his hunch was nothing more than misplaced optimism. Some miles ahead, Reno, his pet Irishman and the rest of his rebel recruits would be in their places and unless the situation changed, the train would speed on through the cutting along its way to the scheduled halt at Knoxville and then on to its final destination of Nashville.

But then came the sign that he had been hoping for, although the source was totally unexpected.

The clergyman occupying the front seat put down his Bible, got to his feet and headed towards the rear of the carriage. It was only when he reached the seats occupied by Ethan and Frank Mason that he paused in his stride. Ethan paid little attention other than to notice that the man appeared to hold Frank's gaze before continuing on his way to the platform outside the carriage.

A couple of minutes passed before Mason eventually spoke. 'Reckon you were right, Cole. You know who that was?'

Ethan shrugged. 'Nope.'

'His name's Dillon and he ain't no minister. He's one of the major's men. You wait here, I'm going outside to see what he's got to say.'

Ethan nodded a silent agreement and watched Mason follow the bogus clergyman to the standing area outside the back of the carriage. He had been right — Reno had not put all his trust in himself and Mason. Instead he had put the fake minister Dillon on the train as a reinforcement.

But Ethan had a feeling of unease. This was not what he had expected and taking orders from Frank Mason did not fit with what he had been told by Daniel Reno before they set out from the farmhouse before sunrise.

'Be careful, Ethan my boy,' he had been told, 'I'm counting on you to keep Frank in order. I am not sure whether I still trust him.'

Ethan eased out of his seat and, making sure that he remained out of sight of the two men outside, he edged his way to within earshot of their conversation.

It was Dillon who was speaking. 'The major knew nobody was going to suspect a minister of carrying guns on board . . . ' Ethan caught a glimpse of the phoney clergyman slipping two six-guns to Mason from under his long black coat. 'So you keep them well hidden until the time comes. And remember your orders, Frank.'

Mason grunted: 'I know my orders, Dillon. And it'll be a pleasure to carry them out. Putting a bullet in that man will be no trouble.'

'Good,' Dillon nodded. 'We don't want Cole to leave this train alive. He's too close to the major so I'm counting on you to make sure that doesn't happen.'

7

Ethan slid back into his seat. Now he knew. As soon as he and Mason, with the help of the guns supplied by Dillon, had forced the engineer to pull the train to its unscheduled halt outside of Knoxville his reward would be a bullet in the back.

He had little time to digest these thoughts before Frank returned to rejoin him. Neither man spoke for several minutes. Ethan realized that Mason was deliberately keeping him in the dark but he allowed him to have his moment before asking: 'You going to let me in on what Reno's messenger boy had to say?'

Mason chuckled. 'Messenger boy? Dillon wouldn't like to be called that, but, yeah, he had a message for us. And something else as well.' He reached inside his shirt, withdrew one of the guns and slid it into Ethan's hand. 'Now, we sit here and we wait.'

'Wait? How do you suppose we are going to get to the engineer without somebody — maybe those two guards up front, spotting us? You planning on shooting everybody in this carriage?'

Mason sniggered. 'You worry too much, Cole. Dillon will take care of that.'

So they waited and Ethan reckoned the train was less than ten minutes out of Knoxville when it happened. The cowboy who had been lounging as if asleep suddenly got to his feet and appeared to stumble, falling into the nearest of the two soldiers.

'Hey, fella! Go steady!' The man in the blue uniform reached out to stop the cowboy from falling but he, too, lost his balance, crashing into his companion. Dillon was on his feet in an instant and, as if on cue, several passengers got to their feet and moved forward to help the others as they tried to keep their balance.

'Come on, Cole, let's go.' Moving swiftly, the pair scrambled out of the rear door and were quickly on to the roof of the carriage. Crouching, they made their way cautiously to the front of the train. With Mason in the lead they were only a few steps from the engine when Ethan reached his decision. Unless he foiled this robbery — and that meant preventing Frank from forcing the engineer to halt the train — he would be lucky to get out of this alive. Mason was planning to kill him. And if he failed there was the fake clergyman Dillon — and no doubt the anonymous cowboy below, to make sure that the job was carried out.

He was edging closer to Mason, his mind on the job of bundling him over the edge and down the embankment below when the first shot came.

Ethan felt the sting as the bullet ripped through his shirt and scorched the skin of his left shoulder. Spinning round, he could see the gunman, another young uniformed soldier, levelling his rifle to take aim and try again. Hindered by the swaying of the speeding train, his second shot was off target. Ethan threw himself flat against the roof of the train, dragging Mason down beside him. All thoughts of dumping Frank over the side were forgotten. Now it was a matter of survival and he needed Mason on his side.

Frank cursed as he was grabbed by the shirt and pulled down.

'Get down!' Ethan snapped. 'We've been spotted. So much for Dillon and his diversion plan.'

Mason did not wait to hear more. He was the kind of gunman who always shot first and if necessary, asked questions later. And he was good at what he did. With a single shot he sent the trooper spinning backwards, his rifle flying off into the air as the young man crashed from his perch.

Mason leaned over the side to watch his victim bounce lifelessly down the bank and into the bushes below.

Scrambling to his knees, he turned to face Ethan. Nobody spoke but the message was clear. One had saved the other's life but there would be no handshake. Instead, Frank signalled that he would go ahead and Ethan's job would be to hold off any more troopers hell bent on heroics. Ethan nodded and watched Mason crawl his way along towards the engine. Up ahead, less than a mile away, Daniel Reno and his gang of train robbers would be waiting.

Ethan knew that the time had come to make his move. What he had overheard changed everything. He had been prepared, if not happy, to go along with the robbery but now his life was at stake and he was only feet away from the man who was an enthusiastic volunteer to put a bullet in him.

Frank reached the back of the wood-filled tender and paused. Below him the fireman and engineer were busy stoking up the locomotive, oblivious of the threat from above their heads.

It was time for Ethan to act but before he could make any move another shot came from behind. He spun round to see that the trooper who had been sent crashing to his death had been replaced by two others. And they were not in the mood to ask questions. It was now a case of kill or be killed. Instinctively, Ethan took aim and fired, wide of the target but close enough to force the two soldiers to duck out of sight.

'This is crazy, Frank,' Ethan yelled above the noise. 'We can't hold them off. If we stop the train now, they'll pick us off for sure.'

'You yeller, Cole?'

It was the sort of sneer he would have expected from Frank Mason but he ignored it. He knew that if a soldier's bullet didn't finish him, Mason would. He was trapped between the two and if he hesitated any longer he was a dead man.

'Dillon's given us up, Frank,' he said desperately. 'How else would they know we were up here?'

It was just enough to cause Mason to pause, and enough time for Ethan to hurl himself at the other man. They tumbled headlong into the piles of wood, the impact knocking much of the breath out of both men. Ethan was the first to recover scrambling to his feet but the advantage was wiped out instantly as Mason lashed out with his boot, the wild kick catching Ethan on the shin.

Mason's gun had spilled from his grasp in the fall but it was within reach when the two men grappled among the logs.

'You bastard, Cole!' Mason cursed. 'I'm gonna kill you.'

'Sorry, Frank, I've got other plans.' Ethan swung his fist flush into Mason's jaw and although the force of the blow sent a searing pain up his arm, it did the trick, sending Frank toppling down the bank of logs and into unconsciousness.

Struggling to his feet, Ethan knew

that his troubles were far from over.
Even though Mason was temporarily
out of the action, there was still Dillon
— and the armed soldiers.

Scrambling across the logs, Ethan
lowered himself on to the footplate and
found himself staring down the barrel
of a rifle.

'That's far enough, mister. One more
step and I'll blow you wide open.'

★　★　★

The craggy soot-stained face of the
engineer was all the evidence Ethan
needed that he was only one wrong
move away from certain death. Slowly
he raised his arms as a token of
surrender.

But his luck was in. The railroad man
was obviously no seasoned gunman and
he clearly felt uneasy holding a man at
gunpoint. Ethan guessed that if he did
nothing to antagonize him he might still
have the opportunity to get out of this
alive.

'Easy, fella,' he said quietly. 'You don't have to fret about me. It's the man up there you have to worry about.'

'Just stay still like I say,' the man snapped. 'Charlie?' He turned to his fireman. 'Get up and check on that critter up there. If he ain't dead, just make sure he ain't no more trouble.'

'What you planning to do, Wes?'

The engineer grunted. 'Sure as hell don't know, Charlie. Can you get back and bring the soldiers? I'll keep this one here. If he makes a move, I reckon it'll be his last.'

'This one's out cold, Wes,' the fireman called after scrambling to Mason's limp figure lying among the logs. 'He's gonna be no trouble.'

The engineer's confidence was growing and he stiffened his grip on the rifle. 'Right, mister. Looks like you got some explaining to do.'

Ethan made to lower his hands but a quick signal with the rifle suggested that would be a bad idea.

'Start talking,' Wes snapped.

But before Ethan could say a word, the fireman, scrambling across the logs towards the back of the tender, suddenly let out a yell of alarm.

'Wes! You gotta stop the train!' The warning shout was enough to force the engineer to turn his head and Ethan took his chance to seize the barrel of the Springfield and drag it from the rail man's grasp.

'Quick, Wes. Stop the train!'

'Best do as the man says,' Ethan said quietly. 'That way nobody else will get hurt. No point in getting yourself shot up for somebody else's gold.'

The engineer backed away, a look of bewilderment on his face. Ethan raised the rifle, a gesture that prompted the man to hurry to apply the brake.

'Don't know who you are, mister, but I reckon you've picked the wrong train — we ain't carrying any gold.'

'Just stop the train,' Ethan told him. 'There's a cutting up ahead. That'll be the place. Do as I tell you and you can walk away from this.'

'As you say, mister,' Wes answered, 'but you're still wrong about the gold. We ain't carrying any gold.'

Charlie was scrambling down from the logs. 'Wes — you gotta stop the train.'

The engineer turned to face his fireman. 'All right, Charlie. I ain't gonna argue with this critter's itchy finger.'

'The hell with him, Wes! Right now we got worse worries.' There was panic in his voice as he pointed frantically at what lay ahead.

The engineer leaned out of his cab and screwed up his eyes to follow the direction of Charlie's pointing finger.

'Holy shit!'

The reaction shocked Ethan. Checking that neither the engineer nor the fireman was any threat, he leaned out of the cab to see what had caused the two railroad men to take fright.

He gasped at the scene up the line that had brought on the panic. Two covered wagons had been driven on to the track to form a blockade. Daniel Reno had taken no chances. It was plain that he had not trusted Mason and Ethan to succeed in carrying out his orders to halt the train and the blockade ahead was a precaution, his guarantee that the train would stop at exactly the spot where his armed men were waiting to board.

Lowering the rifle, Ethan dashed across the footplate. Grabbing the engineer by the arm, he barked: 'Don't stop. Smash those wagons.'

Wes spun round, his face within inches of Ethan's. 'You're crazy man, do you want to get us all killed? I've gotta stop.'

Ignoring Ethan, he spun round and applied the brake. The squeal of the wheels as they gripped the steel rails caused Ethan to lose his footing but he kept his grip on the rifle.

Regaining his balance he looked out to the hillside away to the left of the track. High above, a lone rider sat tall and straight in the saddle, striking in his spotless grey uniform. There was no mistaking the imposing figure of Major Daniel Reno.

Gradually, the train screeched to a halt and Ethan knew that he had run out of time. His chances of preventing Reno's raiders from seizing the train and securing his own survival had gone. No doubt the major had ten, maybe many more armed men ready to climb aboard and butcher the soldiers or anybody who got in their way.

But what had the engineer said? There was no gold on board. Ethan grabbed his wrist as the train shuddered to a stop.

'If there's no gold on board, why all the soldier boys?'

Wes shrugged himself free, no longer worried about the man with the rifle. 'Like I said, we ain't carrying any gold. All we got on board is a few congressmen and the President of the United States.'

★ ★ ★

There was no gold. Daniel Reno had fooled them all . . . Ethan, Frank, the Irishman Rafferty and all the others. His target had never been a bullion haul to fund his crazy plan to re-ignite the dead embers of a lost cause. His ambitions went way beyond the simple matter of a train robbery to pay for the services of a growing group of disillusioned Southerners unable to accept that a peace treaty with the North had ended the four-year conflict and that their lives had changed for ever.

This was one final act of defiance from a mad man. Reno and his troops, poised and waiting up ahead, were planning to kidnap — or kill — Andrew Johnson, the man who had followed Abraham Lincoln into the White House.

Ethan laid the rifle aside. Daniel Reno had often spoken of his admiration for the man he called a hero of the South, the crazy actor John Wilkes Booth who, only four days after the end of the war, had assassinated Lincoln in the Ford Theatre. Now it seemed that Reno was determined to emulate his misguided hero. The kidnap, or the killing, of Andrew Johnson would turn him into a folk hero among the Southerners who still hankered after Jefferson Davis as president and Richmond as their capital city.

The truth had hit Ethan like a stunning blow. This was Daniel's bid for immortality. It was only then, with stark realization that Ethan remembered the date — 15 April, exactly one year on from the very day since the assassination of President Lincoln. It was that sudden awareness of the significance of the day that prompted Ethan into his next move. At the risk of his own life he had to make sure that the train did not stop, that despite the obstruction ahead the train had to smash its way through.

'Listen to me, Wes,' he snapped, grabbing the railway man's shirt. 'I've got no time to explain and you've got no time to think about this. You've got to take this train through those wagons.

If you don't I'm pretty sure your President's going to end up dead. Get this train speeding up again while there's still a chance.'

Leaping from the footplate, Ethan hit the banking with a juddering force that sent pain searing through his body, despite his attempt to soften the fall by bending his knees as he tumbled forward into the gully. Luck was on his side. Heavy rain had left the ground soft so he was able to roll forward out of sight of any soldier who happened to be on hand to see his leap from the train.

Confident that no bones had been broken, he scrambled back up the slope just in time to see that the engineer, whether from panic or trust in what he had been told, had acted on his instructions. The wheels were beginning to roll. But was there enough time for the engine to gather the speed needed to smash the barricade? Suddenly, above the snorting sound of the engine as it gathered speed, came the noise of gunfire. A soldier who had climbed on to the roof of the second carriage, was sent tumbling over the side, his rifle spinning from his grasp and clattering on to the track.

Ethan could see for himself what was happening. From his vantage point high on the hillside, Daniel Reno had seen that the train was gathering speed, that it had no intention of stopping for the wagons blocking the track. He had ordered his men to open fire.

Hurrying forward, crouching in an attempt to stay unseen, Ethan picked up the rifle that had fallen from the soldier's grasp and on to the banking at trackside.

As he watched the train increase speed and head for the barricade, he knew he was now a man alone. Daniel Reno's attempt to assassinate the President of the United States was about to fail and he would know where to turn to point the finger of blame. Ethan was on the run from a one-time friend and soldier who had become a power-crazed madman.

With one final glance at the chaos up ahead, he turned and headed towards the shrubland he hoped would conceal his escape route. For the moment he was safe. As for the future, he knew that Reno would not rest until he had hunted him down and put a bullet in him.

Hidden deep in a cluster of bushes, four other men also watched as the train smashed its way through the improvised barrier. Like Reno, they knew that their plan was in tatters. But while Reno would be putting the blame squarely on the shoulders of Ethan Cole, gambler Jackson Blake was seething that he had paid Frank Mason heavily for failure.

8

The train pulled in to Knoxville just as Frank Mason was stirring from his state of unconsciousness, totally oblivious of the incident that had occurred a few miles down the track. His head ached and as he opened his eyes his vision was blurred; his senses dulled. But he was fully aware that he was staring into the sun-baked features of a US army sergeant.

'Reckon you've got some explainin' to do, mister,' he said, a satisfied smirk breaking up the weather-hardened craggy face. Then he added: 'Before we hang you.'

Frank struggled vainly with the ropes that held his hands strapped behind his back. It was a pointless effort. He was tied to a stiff-backed wooden chair and was surrounded by six, maybe more, blue-clad army men, all, he guessed, willing to be the one who put the rope around his neck.

Mason was not the brightest of men but he could see the hopelessness of his situation. He knew that a stubborn silence would not save his neck from stretching; that there was no reward for loyalty to Daniel Reno. His only hope, and a slim one it was, would be to offer this sneering sergeant his co-operation. Even his help. At least he might then live long enough to get his revenge on that treacherous bastard Cole. And who knows, perhaps the chance of escape might come along.

'Looks like you don't give me much choice, soldier,' he began, 'Maybe if you'd just slacken these ropes we could talk.'

The soldier grinned.

'Now, just so as you know where you stand mister, you talk, and I listen. Then, if I like what I hear I might just loosen those ropes enough for you to scratch your ass.'

'And that's the man's story, sir.'

Andrew Johnson, seventeenth president of the United States and the man who took over from Abraham Lincoln in the White House, had listened without interruption to the report from the congressman who related what he had been told by the sergeant who had questioned the prisoner.

'He said his name was Frank Mason but he was only a hired hand and the real figure behind the attempt was Daniel Reno, his major in the Rebs' army during the war.'

Johnson rubbed his chin thoughtfully. He was angry but, more than that, he was disturbed. And puzzled. As a man of North Carolina and Military Governor of Tennessee at the start of the war he had always had sympathy for the South. His conciliatory policies were opposed by Congress who wanted to keep the Southern states under military government and the new democratic president found himself under attack from hard-line republicans. His unpopularity in Washington was caused by his policy of looking kindly on the states who had formed the Confederacy and threatened to disunite a nation that had known its difficulties and troubles over nearly a hundred years. If there was any truth in the report now being delivered by the congressman there were many Southerners still unhappy that the war was over.

Of course, this man Mason could be lying to save his own skin and Daniel Reno, a name he vaguely remembered from one of the more obscure conflicts of the war, could be a disenchanted renegade unable to accept the new order.

But what if Mason was telling the truth? That there was a latent gathering of disillusioned Southerners eager to return to conflict and that the hatred that had spilled over from the Civil War was about to be re-ignited? It was, the

President reflected, far more likely that Mason and whoever the others were who had tried to board the train at the cutting were under the delusion that they were fighting for a cause and not for the glory of one egotistical ex-soldier.

He walked over to where Frank was tied and spoke for the first time.

'Your friend Daniel Reno has misled you, Mr Mason. There is no gold bullion aboard this train; no potential funds to finance a renewed uprising among Southerners. In fact, though I say this in all due modesty, the only valuable item on this train is myself.' He chuckled, something Andrew Johnson rarely did.

Mason remained silent. Why was he not surprised at this revelation? Why was he not surprised that Reno had led him and the others to believe they were about to become rich when all their reward would be was the hangman's noose as traitors to the new Union? He had often suspected that Reno was not all he pretended. From the day he sent him along with Dutch and Snake to bring Ethan Cole from that backwater hole called Clarkston and then recruiting that crazy Irish drunk Rafferty, there was something about the whole business that didn't ring true. Dutch and Snake were not the sort to take orders by joining any man's army and Rafferty had his own Irish cause to think about.

But it was only now that Frank realized what Reno's true intentions were: the assassination of the president; to become as widely known as that bit actor who had gunned down Lincoln at the end of the war. Well, Mason wanted no part of that. He would hold up trains and banks and stages for one reason only — money. And lots of it. Which was why he had thrown in his lot with that gambler Jackson Blake. Blake was his own kind, a man who took what he needed when he needed it.

Frank studied the men standing over him. A year ago they had been his enemy. He would have happily gunned down each and every one of them in any field in the country. And if Andrew Johnson had been wearing a blue jacket he would have gone the same way. But things had changed — Daniel Reno and others like him were yesterday's men.

'All I can say, Mr President, is that Major Reno was my officer during the war. I felt a loyalty to him, to the cause. I cannot forget that so soon after losing so many friends in battle. What was I to do when he asked me to help?'

The president turned away and called across the soldier who had questioned Mason.

'What's your opinion, Sergeant? Is he telling the truth?'

It took all the soldier's self-control to prevent him from spitting out his disgust.

'Mr President, if you take my advice you won't believe a word he says. He's a reb and they ain't to be trusted, sir. If you want my advice, sir, I'd string him up and let the wolves have what's left.'

Andrew Johnson decided to ignore that suggestion. Instead, he said, 'Maybe before we think about that we might use him to find this man Reno and any others who might be under his influence.'

The soldier gaped at his president with a look of disbelief. He could not believe what he was hearing.

'You're not suggesting we let him go, sir? You can't be.'

'No, not exactly. But we can make a deal. If he helps us to find Reno and get to the truth behind this so-called uprising we could promise him something.'

The president saw the look of horror on the soldier's face and added quickly: 'These deals are done all the time in times of crisis and besides,' he paused and looked across at the man tied to the chair, 'it's not a promise we would have to keep.'

★   ★   ★

Sergeant Gus Kennedy liked the President's thinking. Unarmed and under the watchful eye of six troopers and himself, Mason would do as he was told. He would lead them to Reno and the others — he had mentioned another of the leaders of this failed assassination attempt, a man called Ethan Cole — and after that, well, there would be plenty of open country between there and Nashville for a man to fall from a horse and finish up at the bottom of a gorge.

'You're a lucky man, Mason,' he said reaching down to untie the ropes holding Frank to his chair. President Johnson had rejoined his fellow congressmen in their own private compartment, his final words still lodged in Kennedy's mind. 'We're gonna give you a chance to join the good guys. I'll just tell you I don't believe a word of your rebel lies but I've got my orders. You help me and my men find this Reno and his sidekicks and you get the chance to go free. But, if you're lying like I think you are then I'll save the hangman a job. I'll do it myself. You understand me?'

'Don't worry, soldier, I've got my own reasons for finding that treacherous major and his sidekick Cole. They sold me out so I owe them.'

* * *

The dim light from a distant farmhouse was the only sign of life. Ethan Cole, tired, hungry and battered by the driving rain rose from his crouched position among the bushes. His heartfelt wish was to lie back and close his eyes. But sleep was the last refuge he needed. Soaked to the skin and still unsure of the distance he had managed to put between himself and his pursuers — he had no doubt he was being pursued — he knew he had to go on. But to where? Daniel Reno and his band of rebels would look first towards Clarkston. And when they didn't find him there, what then? Would Alice and the boy be in danger? Was Reno filled with enough hate and anger that his plan to kill the President had been foiled that he would take vengeance against the man he held responsible on an innocent woman and her child?

Ethan had little doubt that if Frank Mason had escaped to rejoin Reno and the crazy Irishman, Dutch and Snake had survived, then his nephew and his brother's widow were in serious danger.

Shaking off as much of the rainwater as he could, he made his decision. The isolated farmhouse must have some method of transportation; he remembered the nearest town was some six miles back and he needed a horse.

He had no intention of harming the occupants of the house but the soldier's rifle he was carrying should be enough to scare them.

There was no need for stealth; the heavy rain would be enough to keep the homesteaders indoors, so when he rose from the ditch he strode purposefully towards the house.

A covered wagon stood at the side of

a small corral; although there was no sign of a horse Ethan knew that if there was a wagon, a horse would be not far away.

He was right. At the back of the house was a small barn where two horses, a chestnut and a pinto, disturbed by the regular banging of the barn door in the strengthening wind, shuffled nervously.

In the dim light, Ethan needed a couple of minutes to locate a saddle. Calming the chestnut with a few soothing pats he was preparing to throw the saddle over the horse's back when, above the sound of the rain and wind, he heard the raised angry voices from inside the house.

He paused, then came the scream following by the crashing noise of shattering glass.

A man yelled, 'Cheating whore!' a woman screeched her own accusation, 'Drunken bastard!' and then another scream.

This was not Ethan's business. He

had to get away, get back to Clarkston to protect Alice and the boy. But could he just ignore the shouting and screaming from inside the house? A man and a woman exchanging curses and screams at each other, a family squabble. Or was it more than that?

There was a lull, only the sound of the wind and rain reaching inside the barn. Then — another scream, followed by a single gunshot.

Ethan abandoned the task of saddling the chestnut, picked up the soldier's rifle and stepped out into the night. The barn was only a few yards from the side of the house but he approached with caution, rifle at the ready. The shouting had stopped.

Rushing up to the house, Ethan pressed his back against the wall and moved furtively into a position where he could peer through the lace-curtained window. Even in the poor light he could make out a table littered with dinner dishes, an upturned broken chair and a shattered lamp. Logs were scattered across the floor in front of the fire grate — all signs of a heated quarrel that had turned vicious.

But there was more concrete evidence of violence. Lying face down, his head turned in a twisted, unnatural angle, his big hands outstretched as if he had been making a desperate grab for something, was a man in a checked shirt. He was motionless. Crouched beside him, rocking to and fro and sobbing hysterically was a young woman. In the space between them was a discarded six-gun.

Ethan made his way to the front of the house and pushed open the door. On the floor, blood seeping from a head wound, was the man he knew as Dutch.

★ ★ ★

A cursory glance was enough to confirm that Dutch was dead. Suddenly the woman stopped sobbing and stared up at Ethan with tear-filled unseeing eyes.

145

'He's dead. I've killed him,' she said, her voice barely above a whisper. 'I've killed my husband.'

Ethan reached down and retrieved the discarded gun.

'What happened?' His voice was soft, encouraging.

'I killed him,' she repeated. 'He wouldn't leave me alone. He kept hitting me, harder and harder. I screamed but he wouldn't stop, just kept saying the others would be here soon. He wouldn't stop. He was drunk, he — ' She burst into tears and the sobbing restarted. She hardly seemed to notice that anybody was there listening to her.

Ethan grabbed her by the shoulders and stopped her rocking.

'The others? What others are coming?'

She didn't reply at first. It was as though she hadn't heard him. The others . . . that could only mean one thing. Snake, the Irishman, perhaps even Daniel Reno himself was on his way. And how many others were still loyal to their major?

'I don't know,' she said at last. 'He was drunk. Always drunk.'

'What is your name?' Ethan asked.

'Angela. Angela van Gerwin. That,' she signalled towards the still form on the floor — 'that is Jan. My husband.'

She was distraught, close to hysteria but Ethan had to work fast. If Reno and the others were heading for this house they had to get away. He could not leave the woman here, nor could he leave Dutch lying in the fire grate. He had to hide the body. But first he had to get the woman back to her senses.

'Mrs — Angela — what's done can't be undone. Your husband's dead and from what you say, you're better he's that way.'

He shook her more violently than he intended but it seemed to bring her out of her trance-like state.

'Who are you? What are you doing in my house?' She was almost at screaming pitch.

'Listen!' Ethan shouted. 'It doesn't

matter who I am or why I'm here. We have to leave.'

'Yes,' she agreed. 'We have to leave, before the others come.' He wasn't sure how much she knew about what was happening but he had no time to worry about her state of mind. He ordered her to collect what she needed, to go out to the barn and saddle the pinto. She stayed silent, nodding as though she understood and then, without a word, turned and left the house and went out into the night rain.

Stuffing the gun into his belt, Ethan reached down and gripped the Dutchman's arm, pulling him up and throwing him across his shoulder. His dead weight was heavier than he expected but he managed to get the body outside with the intention of hiding him in the barn. But then he spotted the covered wagon. That was as good a place as any. Dutch may eventually be found wherever Ethan hid the body but all he could hope for was to buy some time. After the rooms in the house, the barn would be the first place they would look, the wagon hopefully would be the last.

Dumping Dutch into the wagon, Ethan covered the body with a pile of discarded sacks and a blanket. With any luck, it would remain undiscovered for long enough to give them the extra time they would need to make their getaway.

When Ethan eventually reached the barn the woman was standing motionless, staring into the darkness. For the second time he gripped her by the shoulders. There was no time left for soft, soothing words or sweet talk.

'Look!' he snapped. 'Look at me! You can stay here and wait for your husband's friends who are all killers. You understand? Or you can saddle yourself that pinto and come with me. But I am not waiting.' His voice rose with every word as he attempted to emphasize the threat if she remained at the house.

He released her and strode across to the stall where he had left the half-saddled chestnut. It was only when he had completed the task that he turned to notice why the woman had remained unmoved by his chewing out. The pinto was already saddled and ready to ride. Minutes later, without another word passing between them, they were dashing away from the house, away from the dead body of Jan van Gerwin and, if Ethan's judgement was right, away from a group of gun-crazy ex-soldiers.

★ ★ ★

It was in the hour before dawn that the rain finally eased and Ethan decided it was safe enough to take a rest.

'The horses are tired,' he told her. 'They will be of no use. We have to ride them hard and we still have at least a day ahead of us.'

They dismounted, found a sheltered spot away from the wind and settled down.

Eventually it was the woman who

broke the uneasy silence between them. She appeared to have fully recovered from what rage, sorrow or anguish she had suffered when she pulled the trigger to kill her husband.

'I asked you once and you didn't answer me. Who are you? And why did you come to my house?'

It was Ethan's turn to stare into the night. Sooner or later she would have to know and now was as good a time as any other. She could then decide whether to stay with him or go on alone. She might even return to the house she had left behind.

Either way meant little to Ethan. He had made his decision to head back to Clarkston. He had to protect Alice and the boy from Reno and his gang and the best way to do that was to warn them of probable trouble and send her packing to her folks in Union City where they could stay until it was all over.

In the semi-darkness he studied the woman. She was not unlike Alice though maybe a few years older, slimmer but with the same strong features. It was only when she ran a hand through her long uncombed hair that he noticed the bruising under her left eye and the scratch marks across her neck.

'Tell me about tonight,' he said. 'Then I'll explain.'

She looked at him closely. Oddly, she felt at ease in this stranger's company. There were no rough edges to him — unlike most of the men she had ever known in her thirty-three years; he was especially unlike Jan to whom she had been married for six years. He, too, had been a kindly man at first but the war had changed him into a drunken bully, a man filled with hate and greed. A man who had become an outlaw.

'Jan left home two weeks ago and promised me that when he returned we would be rich; we could go anywhere. He even spoke about travelling to Europe to find his family.'

'Did he say how you would get the money?'

She smiled at that.

'Jan never spoke of what he did. All I can say is that he was sober. For the first time since . . . ' she paused as if trying to remember but she didn't continue. Ethan guessed it must have been a long time.

He waited for her to continue.

'He told me that he, he and the others, had been betrayed. They had been ambushed by a group of soldiers because one of them he said was in the pay of the army. I don't know what he meant but he was rambling in drink.

'When I tried to get him to explain he just began cursing, shouting at me, calling me a whore, screaming and hitting me. It was just like before. I don't know what made him do it; he went crazy. I couldn't take any more. When he threw his gun on the table and took his belt, I thought . . . I thought he was going to beat me to death. He couldn't control himself when he had too much drink in him. So, so I picked up the gun and aimed it at him. He just laughed in my face. Called me a worthless bitch and came at me. I — I just pulled the trigger. Next thing I know is that he's lying there in the fire grate. And he's dead.'

Ethan thought she might start sobbing again at that point but she didn't. Instead, she shivered at the memory but said nothing more.

It was Ethan's turn to find out the rest of Dutch's version of the truth.

'Before . . . ' he hesitated, 'did he give you the name of the man he said had betrayed him and his friends.'

The wait for an answer seemed like an age. Then she said: 'He said the treacherous bastard was somebody he had always trusted. Someone who had even been to our home and who I had served a meal. The man's name was Daniel Reno.'

9

Across the county, Daniel Reno slipped quietly into the farmhouse that had been the headquarters for his failed mission to assassinate the President of the United States. It was time to reflect. Time to wonder just how and why his plans had failed. And who was to blame. Could Frank Mason really have been telling the truth, that Ethan Cole, his friend, his trusted captain, had betrayed them at the end. But why?

There had been pandemonium, of course. When the train, instead of slowing had gathered speed and crashed through the barrier of covered wagons, he realized that he had been sold out. The gunfire, the soldiers climbing down from the train; then, hours later at the rendezvous outside Knoxville, Mason scrambling up the slope, gasping the news that Cole had warned the soldiers, breathlessly pleading for Reno to take him up on his horse so that they could make their escape, his men having scattered far and wide as they raced for safety. All were still fresh in his mind, especially the look of horror on the face of Frank Mason when the major, instead of reaching down to help the man up on to the horse, unclipped his holster and fired a bullet straight into the pleading man's heart. He sat and watched him topple back down the slope before turning his horse and heading away.

He gave little thought to the fate of his fellow plotters, men who believed that their sole aim was to relieve the Washington government of hundreds of thousands of dollars in gold bullion to finance a revived Confederacy.

Fools, Reno reflected as he unbuttoned his grey jacket and sagged on to the large bed, sitting and staring at the bedroom floor. Briefly, he wondered if any of them had escaped the bullets of the soldiers. The Irishman, maybe. Dutch? Not Snake, he saw him fall to a blast of bullets when he rushed in and thought he could take on the troopers single handed. The crazy man got what he deserved.

But what about Ethan Cole? There had been no sighting of him. Could he really be the one who turned against him and betrayed the cause?

Reno did not want to believe it but as he lay staring up at the ceiling, he could not escape from the thought that Cole was indeed the culprit. And unless he was told otherwise there was only one course of action he could take. He would hunt down Ethan and kill him. He wouldn't enjoy it . . . at least not until he had told Cole what had really happened the day that his young brother Matthew had died . . .

★   ★   ★

Daniel Reno, a traitor to his own cause? Ethan could not believe that. He had to find out more. What else did Angela van Gerwin know that she wasn't telling him? He found it hard to believe that she knew nothing about Dutch's activities or lifestyle.

Refreshed, they had restarted their journey and the sun was rising into a near cloudless sky. The cold wind and rain of the night were behind them.

'He said that Daniel Reno betrayed him?' Ethan asked, the tone of incredulity suggesting that she must have got things wrong.

But the woman nodded.

'He ranted on about how he had seen with his own eyes that this man Reno had gunned down one of his own men, Frank Mason, and then rode off just as the others were reaching their planned meeting place to tell him that Mason was being followed by some soldiers. I didn't understand any of it.'

So, Frank Mason was dead. Ethan was not sorry to hear that but, killed by the man he eulogized? That came as a shock.

'What happened?'

'Jan and a few others escaped but they split up and scattered.

'When he got home, like I said Jan was out of control. He was raving, drunk and violent, and he kept screaming that they were coming . . . they were coming.'

Ethan pressed her. 'Did he say anything else? Try to remember. It could be important to me.'

She reined her horse to a halt and stared across at him.

'Why is it important? You have to tell me. Why?'

Ethan knew that the time had come to tell her the story. But first he had to know one more thing.

'Did Dutch ever mention anybody else, a man called Ethan Cole?'

She thought for a moment then shook her head. 'Why?'

'I'm Ethan Cole and I was with your husband yesterday.'

★　★　★

Despite Ethan's feeling of urgency that they should put distance between themselves and possible pursuers, they made slow progress on their tired horses. Angela van Gerwin pressed him for more information about her husband's activities and he felt obliged to tell her all he knew. He was, after all, dragging the woman reluctantly away from her home. The least he could give her was an explanation.

He told her how he had met her husband — 'I only knew him as Dutch,' he said, and how he had arrived with Frank Mason and another man known as Snake at the small town of Clarkston to take him to meet Daniel Reno.

'Reno told me and the others we had a part to play in reviving the Confederate cause and part of that plan was to hold up a train carrying gold bullion to Nashville. The war may be over for most people but there are some who won't accept it,' Ethan told her. 'Daniel Reno was one of those men.'

'I can believe my husband would go

along with that. He had never been the same since the war. But what about you?' she asked. 'You don't strike me as a man who would give up his peaceful life to go one a wild boar chase.'

'I owed Daniel Reno,' Ethan told her. 'He saved my life in the war.'

Angela sensed there was more to it than that but she let it ride.

'And what happened at the train?'

Ethan let out a weary chuckle. 'Let's say I don't owe Reno any more. And there's no Southern unrest or Confederate conspiracy . . . just a bitter and twisted old soldier hell-bent on writing his name in history. There was no gold on that train — just the President of the United States. Daniel Reno sent us there to set up the assassination of Andrew Johnson.'

The woman took it all in before saying: 'So that's why Jan said Daniel Reno was a traitor?'

'I guess so,' Ethan said. 'And unless I'm mistaken Reno isn't finished yet . . .'

Daniel Reno slept fitfully but by daybreak he was awake and fully focused again. The chance to make his mark on history had gone. Andrew Johnson would see through his term of office as US President, Washington would remain the capital and Southern loyalists like him would become the forgotten men of the age. But not before he had settled a score.

He would need men, of course. Frank was gone, he was sorry about that, but he would have made a hostile witness if things ever got that far. He expected Dutch to have got away, probably headed for that neat little farmhouse he had set up with that pretty wife of his. Daniel could start there. It would be good to see her again. Perhaps she would be more accommodating this time, especially if Dutch was full of whiskey again.

But first he would try to find that mad Irishman and his friends again. He was fairly sure they would not have hung around and got themselves shot to pieces. He didn't need Snake; the man was a jackass and if he got in the way of a few soldiers' bullets no harm was done. But maybe another gun or two would come in handy.

Trouble was, they would need paying this time. Not in promises of gold but in hard cash. Now that Mason had gone to meet his Maker he doubted that any of them knew the truth behind the raid on the train but he was not as sure that they would trust him again without seeing the colour of his bills. Especially Martin Rafferty. The Irishman would need some evidence this time.

Daniel bathed and shaved and took meticulous care to hang his neatly pressed army uniform on the specially designed tailor's dummy before dressing in the grey civilian suit which made him an easily recognized figure around town. Later, when the time came, he would change again into the more familiar livery of a cowpuncher, a gun on each hip and his uniform neatly packed in his saddle roll for the coup de gras moment — Daniel could never totally abandon his eccentricities — for the ride to Clarkston and the payday for Ethan Cole.

He checked his necktie, his slicked down silver hair and the neat fit of his coat. Then, with a quick glance around, he left the room.

His sister, Sarah Tomkins, was busily preparing food when he entered the small cooking area of the house's kitchen.

'I may be away some time, my dear,' he told her. 'I have important business in town that may take me some days to complete. But when I return we will discuss arrangements for you to open that small tea house and café you always spoke about. Maybe in Chatta-nooga.'

Sarah smiled but it was nothing more than a gesture. Her brother had made many promises but rarely delivered on any of them. This one would be no different, but could she simply walk out and leave him, catch a train or a stage ride and make a life for herself in Chattanooga as they had suggested many times?

Ever since the death of his father so many years ago, Daniel had lived life like a man without soul. There was bitterness in him, something she had never known while they were children.

She no longer knew anything of his life except that, much to her alarm, he appeared to have a death wish. She had often heard, through the thinness of the house walls, his nightmare ramblings followed by endless pacing of his bedroom floor.

By day he was back to his normal buoyant and confident self, just like this morning, but as she watched him climb aboard the buggy and slap the horse into action to set off for town she could not help wondering what dark secrets he was storing up inside.

As the buckboard disappeared among

the row of trees, Sarah returned to her cooking and said a silent prayer.

★ ★ ★

News of the abortive train raid had spread throughout the town to produce a string of wildly extravagant rumours about the intentions of the would-be raiders.

'What's your view of the incident, Major, you being a military man of some standing? I suppose you have heard about it?' Daniel was asked as he drew to a halt near the newspaper office.

'Who can see into the minds of such people?' he offered. 'Fortunately, I understand the President and his, er, entourage of congressmen escaped unharmed. That is a relief I'm sure.'

'A fortunate relief indeed,' the newspaper man agreed. 'A serious incident, especially in these parts, would not go down too well up in Washington. Do you know, Major, there are still some

166

folk in government who would treat Southerners, and especially former Confederate soldiers like your good self, as second class citizens.'

'So I understand,' Reno said and walked on.

His first call was at the small gambling hall and bar across from the courthouse. If Rafferty wasn't there, even at this time of day, he would not be far away. But he was not disappointed. The Irishman was in the room, a spectator at a dice game. And he was sober. However, he did not seem too pleased to see the major striding across the floor. The men exchanged brief cold stares before Reno eventually broke the ice with the semblance of a smile.

'You look well, my friend,' he said, ignoring the strange looks of the gamblers at the dice table.

'Bejasus! It's not thanks to you now, is it?'

But Reno had not come for an argument.

'Perhaps not, Martin, but we do have

167

some unfinished business I would like to discuss with you to our mutual benefit.'

Anybody listening in or simply eavesdropping the major would have no hint of the matter under discussion; they would simply assume they were overhearing another of the major's condescending lectures to a man he had rescued from a spell in prison a few days earlier. The people of Knoxville had already dismissed the previous day's abortive raid as the work of out of county outlaws. Daniel Reno was a respected man around town which meant that, despite the obvious coarseness and vulgarity, the Irishman, by association, was to be at worst ignored or avoided.

'I suggest we take a seat in the corner and talk, my friend,' Reno said, removing his hat and dropping it on to a table. 'Over a drink or two, like good friends.'

'So it's friends are we?' Rafferty snapped, still unwilling to abandon his aggressive attitude.

Reno slid into a chair and waited. He could understand the Irishman's reluctance but he needed him.

Eventually, and reluctantly on the part of Rafferty, they sat down. They talked, and ten minutes later Reno had persuaded the other that there was still a prize to be won and with the added bonus of revenge on the man who had betrayed them and cost the lives of his friends.

Satisfied, Reno left the rooms and headed down the street to the bank. Now was the time to use his status as an upstanding member of society worthy of the trust of the bank manager — and a $5,000 loan.

He would need it, not for the purchase of prize livestock as he would tell the manager, but to pay for the services of the Irishman and the others in advance. Then, an unscheduled withdrawal from the Clarkston bank would bring them a good return. The train raid may have failed and Andrew

Johnson may be back in his presidential bed in Washington but somebody had to pay for that.

Ethan Cole and the people of a sleepy little South Tennessee town would be the ones to pay. Daniel Reno was not a man to forgive or forget. By nightfall he, along with Martin Rafferty, Tex Dillon and a fourth man Dillon had vouched for were on their way to Clarkston.

★ ★ ★

Reno and his men were setting out from Knoxville when Ethan Cole and Angela van Gerwin reached the first of the small farmhouses that ringed the small town.

The long journey had been tiring and Ethan found himself feeling sorry for the woman. He knew she had agreed to ride along with him only because she was terrified of the law discovering she had killed her drunken husband, even though it was a killing in self defence.

He also felt that she could see the truth of this stranger's story, that her husband had been a brute, probably a killer and a thief. A man who would happily swallow the idea that he was about to become rich by relieving a train of its gold bullion. But, to kill the president? Jan van Gerwin, a Dutch immigrant who had chosen the Confederacy as his flag of convenience and regular pay during the Civil War, would have no part in that. If there was no gain he did not care a cent who ran a country that was not his own. Had the realization that he had been duped into a fruitless raid been what sent him into a drunken rage?

She would never know.

Ethan also reckoned, hoped even, that she could see the honesty in him. No doubt she had been fooled before by men full of promises that came to nothing.

He studied her carefully. Had she recovered from the hysteria that had overcome her at the sight of her husband lying dead at her feet? But, as the first dim lights of town came into view it was time to put that behind him and try to plan ahead. He knew by now that Reno would have gathered enough guns to form a search party.

★ ★ ★

It was Rafferty who pulled back the sacking and saw the body.

'It's your man Dutch,' he said, dropping the cloth. 'Bullet hole in him.'

Reno cursed, something he rarely did. He was proud of his vocabulary and he looked on cussing as a weakness of character, something for uneducated men such as the three now accompanying him. They had arrived at the house fully expecting Dutch and his wife to be enjoying an evening meal. Instead the house was deserted; the fire in the grate dead and signs of a struggle in the form of a broken chair and upturned table.

It was only when the search of the house and the empty barn revealed

172

nothing that the Irishman looked inside the covered wagon to find Dutch's body.

'Cole's been here,' Reno said to nobody in particular. 'I can feel it. And he's taken Dutch's woman with him.'

'And why would he do that, Major? Would you be telling me that?'

Reno smiled. 'Believe me, Martin, when I tell you, you don't know any men like Ethan Cole. He knew I would be coming after him and I would call here to collect Dutch. If he killed our friend as it seems, he could not leave the woman here.'

'He could have just killed her.'

The smile vanished from Reno's face and he glared at the Irishman.

'As I said, my Irish rebel friend, Ethan is not like men you would know. He does not kill people, especially a woman, just to satisfy himself. No. He will have taken the woman with him. Even though it would slow him down.'

It was Dillon's turn to speak. 'As you say, Major, she would slow him down. So why?'

'Because I know where he is going. And he will know that I know.' He strolled purposefully towards the house. 'You have all been paid half of what you are getting to do this job. The rest will come when it is over. Meantime, there is no hurry. I suggest we all take advantage of our departed Dutch friend's hospitality and get some sleep. And I'm sure there will be something in the food store for us to have a good breakfast before we set off for Clarkston.'

★　★　★

The reunion was tearful. Alice Cole cried at the sight of her dead husband's brother striding up the path towards the house; Jonathan cried, too, but his were tears of joy. Together they hurried to the door and together they rushed out to greet the homecomer. Neither seemed to notice the woman who had still not dismounted from her horse.

'Hey, easy you two, you'll have me in tears.' Ethan lifted the boy with one hand and put his arm around his sister-in-law. 'I've only been away a few days.'

'But you're home now,' said Alice and then, for the first time she acknowledged the presence of another woman.

Ethan released her.

'Alice, this is Angela. She's er . . . well let's all go inside and we can talk about it.'

Alice's puzzled frown was enough to tell Ethan that he would have to tread carefully with his explanation. He would have to convince both women to take Jonathan to a safe place until he sent for them. He knew he would have to tell Alice and Jonathan why but right now he was hungry. And with an Alice Cole breakfast inside him things might look a little brighter.

★　★　★

'I'm not leaving my house!' Alice's protest was almost a shout. 'I won't do it.'

Ethan sighed. 'Please, Alice. I've told you what will happen when Reno and his men come.'

'I'll take that chance. This is my home. I am not going to be run out of it by some crazed ex-soldier. The war is over, Ethan. It's time to put it behind us.'

'Everything you say is true,' he said, 'but that won't stop Daniel Reno from coming here with the sole purpose of killing me. He believes I betrayed him and he won't forget that. I know I am asking a lot of you but . . . think of Jonathan. Reno is not the sort of man who will spare your son. Even if I leave he will take his hate out on you before coming after me. I'm begging you, go to your sister's in Union City. Take Jonathan and Angela with you. I'll come for you when it is all over. If he — ' his voice faded.

'If he kills you, that's what you were going to say, isn't it? Since I lost Matthew you have been like a father to Jonathan and . . . a good friend to me . . . and now you are telling me that a man you once served and admired is bringing a gang of men to town to kill you.'

Ethan played his final card. The only ace he had left.

'Alice, if I have only myself to worry about I can stop Reno and his men.'

'You don't even know how many there will be,' she interrupted. He gripped her wrists across the table.

'Alice, I'm begging you . . . please go to your sister's.'

She suddenly burst into tears. 'Ethan, you must know . . . I have never been able to say this before but . . . ' she stumbled with the words that she could not bring herself to say. She was in love with her dead husband's brother.

'We'll talk about it later, when you come back from Union City.' It was then that the door burst open and Angela van Gerwin and a laughing Jonathan burst into the room. The boy was waving a new toy, the result of an early morning visit to a new store in town, and was laughing like any other child without a care in the world.

'Mom, look what Mrs Angela bought me,' he said thrusting the wooden horse into his mother's lap. She looked down at her wide-eyed son and she decided.

'Jonathan, how would you like to take a trip to Aunt Lucy's in Union City — just for a few days?'

He stared up at her.

'Will Uncle Ethan come, too?'

'No, but Mrs Angela can come if she wants to.'

Ethan turned and glanced at Dutch's widow. She nodded.

'I'd love to go with you, Jonathan.'

10

Daniel Reno studied the three men seated around the table outside the small trading post where they had stopped on the road to Clarkston. He had hand-picked them, except for the one who said his name was Jake Regan, and, after some well chosen words of persuasion he was convinced they could be relied upon to carry out his instructions. Reno was used to giving orders and having them obeyed. It came naturally to an army man. He expected things to be no different now that they were all out of uniform.

The trading post manager produced the four steaks and coffee mugs that had been ordered and left them to their meals.

But Daniel Reno was more interested in talking than eating as he watched the motley trio attack their food. Rafferty, in his own strange way, was loyal, especially when there was money involved. He would enjoy robbing a bank, which meant he had to be watched carefully once the job was done.

Dillon, a thin, sour-faced Texan spoke very little but listened a lot — the sort of man Reno liked to have by his side. Silent and obedient. No soldier could ask for more from his men.

He had still to find out if the burly one called Regan had any qualities, other than an ability to use a gun, that he could use in future. He had already decided that Regan would be the man he would send into town with instructions.

Reno pushed his untouched plate to one side. He reached inside his coat and pulled out a bundle of dollar bills which he threw in Regan's direction.

The others paused in mid-bite and stared across the table.

Reno exhaled a sigh of satisfaction.

'So now that's got your attention,

gentlemen, we talk about how we are going to empty the bank at Clarkston and I am going to get Ethan Cole to pay for his crimes.'

★　★　★

Jesse Lassiter had been sheriff for only a few weeks but he was already feeling that he was born to wear the star.

Clarkston was a small, close-knit and law-abiding community and the peace officer's job rarely called for anything more demanding than issuing a serious lecture on a Saturday night, usually to one of the five or six regular offenders all the worse for lengthy drinking sessions in Fitzgerald's Saloon.

The job also offered Jesse the time to think seriously of his future. He had lived in and around the town for all of his twenty-eight years, helping first on his father's small farm before taking a job with the South Tennessee Stage Company. When old Ben Dawson decided that it was time to turn in his badge the opportunity came to earn himself a steady job as a lawman. There were no objectors when Jesse put his name forward and he was duly sworn in as the law officer responsible for Clarkston and the surrounding district.

But much more important to Jesse Lassiter than keeping the peace among the Clarkston drunks was the fact that he would see a lot more of that pretty widow Alice Cole. Jesse had always admired her, ever since they bumped into each other on the boardwalk outside her brother-in-law's general store but he lacked the courage and self-belief to approach her. Now that he was a leading figure in the town he felt the time was right to shake off those self-doubts and make his attentions known. Now he could offer her a settled home and a secure future.

He liked young Jonathan, though he had never been too friendly with the boy's father, Matthew Cole.

Jesse knew that she had not been

walking out with any man since her husband was killed in the war although her storekeeper brother-in-law had been keeping a protective eye on her. But his protection and guidance would no longer be needed if Jesse played his cards right. Today was that day and as he wiped away the remains of the soap after finishing his shave and checking his appearance he stepped out into the sunlit morning and headed towards the neat house at the end of the main street.

'Good morning, Sheriff. Fine day.'

That was Silas Jones, the bank manager. Jesse had never had much dealing with him although he had heard stories . . . and they involved a certain gambling house and a woman whose reputation ruled out any possibility that she would ever be known as a lady. But that was no business of a young lawman so Jesse simply nodded, touched the brim of his hat and walked on.

Only a few steps further along the street, 'Good morning, Jesse. Don't forget, there's a meeting tonight.'

The sheriff touched his hat again. 'I won't forget, Mayor. I'll be there.'

He knew exactly why Mayor Buckle wanted him along at the town meeting. His test period as sheriff was over and it was time to talk about his pay and the appointment of a deputy. Jesse knew he had made a good impression on the mayor and his fellow council members and he had already picked out a candidate for the deputy's job. Life was good. Even the townswomen's committee approved of the handsome young man who had stepped into the boots of Ben Dawson.

Jesse strolled enthusiastically towards the house at the end of the street. Things could not get much better. All he needed now was for Alice Cole to accept his invitation to the Saturday night party in the church garden.

Easing open the low white picket gate, the sheriff felt he was walking on air as he strode up the short footpath leading to the door. But he was instantly deflated when his knocking was answered, not by the woman had had come to sweet talk but by a man he thought had left town — maybe for good.

'Ethan!'

'Jesse Lassiter. What can I do for our new sheriff?'

The young lawman felt all the confidence he had struggled to find for this visit draining away.

'I was calling to see Alice . . . Mrs Cole,' he said nervously. For a man who had reached the age of twenty-eight, he was surprisingly unworldly in the ways of courtship and that situation wasn't helped when Ethan offered a knowing smile. Or was he imagining that? Was it simply a friendly smile for a visiting neighbour?

He was close to becoming flustered with uncertainty when Ethan said: 'Alice and Jonathan are out of town for a few days, visiting her sister in Union City.'

Jesse regained his composure.

'Isn't that kinda sudden? She never said anything when I saw her yesterday.'

It was Ethan's turn to become puzzled. Why was Jesse calling so early in the morning? Did he look like a man who had come courting, or was there some other reason the sheriff would call on a pretty widow?

Ethan wondered whether it was any of his business but now the man was at the door, maybe it would be time to tell him the reason for Alice's sudden departure. The day would come soon when he would need the law on his side because he had no doubt that when Daniel Reno did come looking for him there would be gunplay.

'You should come inside, Sheriff. We need to talk.'

*   *   *

The bank's first customer of the day arrived moments after Silas Jones opened the doors. The manager smiled a welcome to the burly grey-suited stranger, a figure of affluence if ever Silas saw one.

The man introduced himself as Nelson Monroe. It was Daniel Reno's idea to combine the hated names of the brigadier general who was Jefferson Davis's jailer, Miles Nelson, and the Virginia prison where the president of the Confederacy was imprisoned, Fortress Monroe, and Regan felt the name suited his invented status as a rich railroad and landowner.

Reno rightly assumed that nobody among the town's farmers, ranchers and mill workers would know of either man or prison and when the time came they would read about the robbery and wonder how they had failed to notice anything suspicious at the time.

'And what can we do for you this fine morning, sir?' Silas said in his finest grovelling tones. Regan liked that, the only time anybody had spoken to him with respect was when they were looking down the barrel of his six-gun. He went into his well-rehearsed speech.

'Well, mister — did I get your name?'

'Jones. Silas Jones. I'm the manager of this bank.'

Regan studied his surroundings. The room was smartly furnished with leather seating, a wide oak-topped desk and, a row of cabinets and a regular safe. Alongside that was a locked barred gate and beyond, Regan noticed, the main attraction — a giant safe and strong room. Two young clerks were busy at their positions waiting for the day's first business.

Regan leaned forward and rested his elbows on the desk, a conspiratorial pose that prompted Silas to follow the lead and move closer.

'I guess you've heard my name, Mr Jones. Nelson Monroe. The railroad family.'

'Of course,' Silas lied. He did not wish to appear ignorant in the presence of a man who clearly had money and influence. 'The railroad people.'

Regan was warming to his role. 'I trust that what I am about to tell you will remain between ourselves. It is, as they say in our circles, Silas, a very delicate matter.'

From that moment Regan had the old bank manager in the palm of his hand. Just as Reno had promised, flattery would do the trick.

When he eventually left the bank and headed towards the hotel, Regan had all the information he needed.

He had spun the gullible bank manager a story about his company's plans to bring their new rail link through Clarkston and how he would need the security of a reliable bank to safeguard the large payrolls that would be coming into town. And Silas had told him everything he needed. His personal tour of the bank's facilities had confirmed all he wanted to know; the security was in the hands of two young clerks, Jones himself and an occasional visit from the sheriff.

'But I assure you, Mr Monroe, your money will be safe with us. Clarkston is a small, law-abiding community. I am sure that any strangers in town would be challenged by our sheriff, Jesse Lassiter. He is a very keen young man who has just got his star so, believe me, your company is making a wise choice coming to us.'

Regan remembered the $2,000 Reno had given him to use as his sign of good faith by opening an account but, in his haste to please, Silas asked for no such security from his new customer. Jake Regan was $2,000 richer — he felt no obligation to return the money to that red-eyed rebel.

He was crossing the street when he caught sight of the lawman Silas Jones had spoken about. He was heading Regan's way and his young features were set grimly. He had clearly had some unwelcome news, as he strode purposefully towards his office.

Regan allowed himself a private smile; if the sheriff thought he was having a bad day now, what would he think once Reno and his men had made their return visit?

*　*　*

Jesse Lassiter sat at the back of the small room and listened to the town's elders discussing him and his job. He was happy at what he was hearing but his delight was tempered by what was to come. And that followed his talk with Ethan Cole that morning.

Eventually, Mayor Buckle nodded in his direction, a signal that he could say his piece.

'Looks like the town's got itself a permanent sheriff, Jesse. How d'you feel about that?'

He had listened to the men at the table discussing his first four weeks as the town's lawman and, apart from bar owner Carl Fitzgerald questioning his ability to deal with anything more serious than a drunken skirmish — a worry that was instantly dismissed by a ripple of laughter because nothing worse ever happened in Clarkston — the nodding heads were in agreement. Jesse Lassiter was without doubt the man for the job.

He stood up and faced the men responsible for the confirmation of his appointment and looked into the faces of the town council.

Then he said, 'I am happy to carry on as town sheriff, Mr Mayor, but I think you ought to hear what I have to say.'

All five men stared back at the young man with the star.

'The town may soon be visited by a group of rebel soldiers with murder in their hearts.'

The men at the table remained silent, exchanged puzzled glances and then left it to Mayor Buckle to say, 'Can you explain that, Jesse?'

'They're coming for Ethan Cole,' he said but that did nothing to clear up the mystery so Buckle waved at him to continue.

'I called on Mrs Cole this morning only to find that she had left town to visit her sister in Union City and in the house was Ethan — '

'Ethan?' somebody interrupted. 'I thought he'd left town.'

'He's back,' said Jesse patiently, 'and he's on the run from some of his one-time army friends.'

He then related the story as he had been told it by Ethan.

The failed attempt by Daniel Reno's gang of dissident rebel soldiers to rob a train and assassinate President Andrew Johnson brought gasps of disbelief from the pople gathered around the table.

But Ethan had lied on one major point — his own part in the plan to derail the train. He had told Jesse that he had been there purely by chance, that he was a passenger on the Nashville-bound train carrying Johnson and his entourage and that his involvement had been to help save the life of the President.

The mayor held up his hand to interrupt Jesse's report.

'So why does Ethan believe that these men are coming for him?'

The sheriff continued his story.

'He told me that during the shoot-out he came face to face with this man Reno. During the war, Ethan Cole was one of his officers and his young brother Matthew, Jonathan's father and Alice Cole's husband' — he paused to emphasise the connection — 'was in his troop. Seems, Mr Mayor that this man Reno saved Ethan's life and tried to save Matthew when he was shot in the back. They were close friends until the end of the war when Ethan came back to Clarkston to take over the general store.'

Mayor Buckle slapped the table. 'You still haven't told me why this Reno wants to come after Ethan.'

Jesse remained calm. 'Because when the two men came face to face during the skirmish he threatened to hunt Ethan down and kill him. Called him a traitor to the cause and said he would not let him rest until he got his revenge.'

The lawman paused before adding, as if reluctantly, 'The thing is, Mr

Mayor, I'm not sure he was telling the whole truth. From what I understand, Ethan left town to meet with an old army colleague. Now, I wonder, who could that be? If it was this Reno fella it means that he wasn't there by chance — he was part of the hold-up team.'

The room fell silent. Ethan Cole, one of the town's most liked figures, was in danger. A group of rebels was coming to town to kill him. Clarkston was a small peaceful town that knew nothing of outlaws and killers. Indeed, only an hour earlier, Silas Jones had reported that a man called Nelson Monroe had paid him a visit with a view to investing in his bank because there were plans to build a railroad through the town. That would bring prosperity to the small community. The mayor had been impressed. Now he was angry.

'I can't believe that, Jesse. Not Ethan. The question is, what do you plan to do about it?'

'Yeah, what you going to do, Sheriff?'

The question came from Fitzgerald, the man who had doubted Jesse's ability to deal with any trouble beyond a drunken brawl.

'Until something happens there isn't much I can do,' Jesse said. 'Ethan may be worrying too much.'

'He's worried enough to send his brother's widow and her son out of town,' Fitzgerald argued, still not satisfied. 'And how much do we know about this man Reno?'

The council members exchanged puzzled glances and shook their heads.

'Maybe we should ask Ethan about him?' Silas Jones suggested.

'Now just hold on a minute, gentlemen!' The booming voice came from the back of the room and Jesse had to turn to catch a glance of the speaker. The Reverend Joshua Tullett stepped forward. 'I realize I am no more than an onlooker at these proceedings and my own province is the pulpit on a Sunday but may I make a suggestion that would suit all?'

The mayor nodded in the minister's direction.

'Go ahead, Reverend. What do you suggest?'

'Mr Jones has already told us of the visit he had from the railroad man and his intentions for our town. In view of that, I believe the last thing Clarkston needs right now is a serious disturbance of its peace. Maybe we cannot stop this Major Reno and his men from coming to town but perhaps we can do something to prevent bloodshed. We must convince Mr Cole that he should leave town.'

The suggestion brought a shocked silence from the council members until Mayor Buckle broke in. 'Reverend, you are a comparative newcomer to our little community and no doubt full of good intentions. I have heard your sermons,' that brought a chuckle around the table, 'but I have to say this. Ethan Cole and his family have lived here all their lives. We are in no position, nor would we wish to be, to, how can I put this? run him out of town. Ethan is entitled to the full protection of the law and it is up to Sheriff Lassiter here to provide exactly that.'

There were murmurs of approval and Reverend Tullett resumed his seat at the back of the room.

The mayor turned to Jesse. 'Now, Sheriff, the matter is in your hands. If you need any help, you just have to ask. You have our permission to appoint deputies as you wish.'

Jesse thanked him. There were just two problems but he kept them both to himself. There was no knowing when Reno would arrive in town. And he wasn't sure how much he wanted to keep Ethan Cole alive . . .

* * *

Silas Jones left the meeting early with the excuse that he had enough work to keep him occupied for most of the night. It was the night that four masked men broke into the bank, emptied its safes and bludgeoned the luckless manager into unconsciousness. But before the gun butt smashed down on to his skull the man who was clearly the leader of the group spoke softly and menacingly in his ear.

'You can count yourself extremely lucky, Mr Bank Manager. I am sparing you so that you will be able to tell Mr Ethan Cole that he can expect a visit very soon.'

11

George Callaway examined his handiwork and nodded with satisfaction.

'You'll live, Silas,' he said. 'Though I wouldn't go round head-butting any doors for some time.'

The bank manager struggled to his feet, gingerly fingered his bandaged head.

'Thanks, Doc. I'll be fine.'

Callaway re-packed his medical bag and left Silas Jones and the others, Mayor Buckle, the reverend, the sheriff and the newspaperman James Kerring to discuss the events of the previous night.

'You reckon it was this Reno fella then, Silas?' The mayor pressed. 'You sure about that?'

'No, I ain't sure, Mayor. All I can tell you is what he said. That he's coming for Ethan Cole. And he's coming soon.'

'Anything else, Silas? Anything that might help me?'

It was Jesse who posed the question but Silas grimaced as he felt the stabbing pain from the blow to the head brought on by his rising irritation that he had to keep repeating himself.

'Nothing, Jesse, except, well . . . one of them was a loudmouth. And he was Irish. I'm sure of it. They wore masks but he didn't wear a hat, just a shock of red hair. The boss yelled at him before he hit me. Called him Martin.'

Kerring had been busily scribbling notes, filling the *Clarkston Informer* would be no trouble this week. A bank robbery, the manager accosted and the threat of an attack on one of its most popular citizens — it was the sort of news he would secretly dream about but never admit. He stopped writing.

'What you planning to do about this, Sheriff?' he said turning to face Jesse.

The young lawman looked nervously first at the injured bank manager and then at the mayor.

'What do you suggest? I can hardly go chasing all over the country looking for four masked men now, can I, Mr Kerring?'

'Well, we can't just sit around and wait for them to come back for Ethan Cole, can we?' the newspaperman sneered.

'We've got to persuade him to leave town right away,' the clergyman repeated the suggestion he had made at the council meeting.

'Whatever we do I'm gonna need some deputies,' Jesse said after a short silence. For an hour the five men tried to find a solution to their problem.

'We could always barricade the main street,' Kerring said eventually, his thoughts more on another front page for the *Informer* than on the welfare of the town and its citizens.

It was only when the mayor eventually delivered his suggestion that the group came to an agreement.

'This bank robbery changes things, gentlemen. Silas, here, had his life put in danger and if we let these robbers back into town we can be sure they won't stop with Ethan Cole. They are no respecters of law and order.' He paused then added, 'Perhaps the reverend is right. Maybe we should tell Ethan to leave town. I will go with the sheriff and put it to him. I'm sure he will see it's the wisest thing.'

There were nods of approval all round. That would be the best thing to do.

'And what if he doesn't agree to that?' Lucas Kerring asked.

The mayor chuckled. 'Then I guess we get Jesse to run him out of town.'

Nobody was sure whether he was serious . . .

★   ★   ★

Daniel Reno knew he would have to keep a careful watch on the Irishman and the new man Regan. They were already heavily liquored up after the bank raid and he needed them sober for the second part of the job in hand. After that — they could do what the hell they wanted. Rafferty had already forced him into one stupid mistake — giving away his name during the bank robbery.

It was almost dawn before the pair eventually fell into a drunken sleep and Reno decided it was time to take the Texan into his confidence. He had known Dillon briefly in their few days together as law students in Memphis. Neither had taken to the law as a career, instead looking to the military for their futures. That life had appealed to Reno but Tex Dillon became a drifter until the pair eventually teamed up again in the first year of the war.

The four men had made camp five miles out of Clarkston, well off the main track and away from any passers-by or prying eyes and while the others drank heavily and counted their share of the robbery Daniel Reno spent the night hours deep in thought.

The time had come when he had to

admit to himself that his army days were behind him and the failure to rid the world of Andrew Johnson, for which Ethan Cole would pay heavily, was not the way he would have chosen to put his grey uniform away for the final time. But the longer he sat and the more he reflected, Reno's thoughts moved towards a new, appealing venture. He never lost the belief in himself — that he was born to lead. And if the army could no longer accommodate a man of his talents in a position of power, perhaps it was time to create his own.

Clarkston was a quiet town, full of small-town minds. He had learned that the town was to become a rail depot and Regan had convinced them he was the man responsible for the project. It was the sort of place Reno and his chosen troops could use as a base. A young sheriff would offer no resistance in the face of Rafferty, Regan, Dillon and Reno himself. The town was theirs for the taking. As he sipped his coffee

Reno was warming to the idea. The bank robbery would have scared the good folk of Clarkston. Perhaps their small, isolated Tennessee homes were not as safe or secure as they had always believed. He would offer to protect the town and they would accept.

Yes, he thought, I will make Clarkston my own. Once that treacherous Ethan Cole was out of the way.

'You got any plans when we're through, Tex?' Reno asked, passing his friend a coffee mug.

The other shrugged. 'Nothing special. You got something in mind?'

Reno had a lot in mind. And he told the Texan about it.

Dillon enjoyed hearing how he would become a sheriff, and how Rafferty would run the only saloon while Regan would take care of the women who would flock into town. And he agreed that Daniel Reno would be an excellent mayor.

It was then that Reno settled down to enjoy a couple of hours' sleep before drawing up the final plans to deal with Ethan Cole.

* * *

Ethan wiped his face, ran his fingers across his newly-shaven chin and checked in the mirror for any traces of blood. There were none.

Satisfied, he pulled on his shirt, buckled his belt and lifted his hat from its hook behind the door. It was time to pay young Jesse Lassiter a visit.

He had been less than impressed by the sheriff's cool response to his request for the help of the law the previous day. He explained how he expected Daniel Reno to come after him following the way he had helped to sabotage the attempt on the President's life; and how Jesse would do his career and reputation no harm by putting Reno behind bars and sending for a circuit judge.

'How many men will he have?'

Ethan shrugged. 'Three, maybe four. Reno's a conceited and arrogant man and he will think that will be more than enough to handle a small town greenhorn sheriff and a couple of raw deputies.'

'There's no deputies. Just me.'

'And me,' Ethan said but he was far from convinced that the young lawman's heart was in the job ahead.

He had not reached the end of the short path leading from Alice's house when he spotted the sheriff approaching. And he had company. Mayor Buckle was striding purposefully in front followed by Lassiter and a man Ethan recognized as the owner of the *Clarkstown Informer*. They looked as though they had serious business in mind.

It was the mayor who broke the news to Ethan.

'The bank was robbed last night. Silas was hurt.'

Ethan avoided putting forward the question they were waiting for him to ask.

'We think it was your friend, Reno,'

the newspaper man put in. 'Silas said he left a message — that you could expect a visit. And soon.'

Ethan studied the three men closely. The mayor was clearly uncomfortable; the sheriff was also ill at ease but Kerring had the look of a man enjoying the discomfort of everybody else.

'How many were there?' he asked.

'Silas reckons there were four of them. They were all masked but he said one of them was a loudmouth Irishman. What you told Jesse here, it sounds like Reno's work.'

'That was Reno's men. The Irishman's a hothead by name of Rafferty. I already told the sheriff he'd be here soon,' Ethan said. 'I didn't reckon on him robbing the bank except — ' his voice tailed off.

'Except what?' Buckle asked impatiently.

'He's got to pay his henchmen and what better way to do that than empty a small town bank? I reckon he'll be back sooner than I thought, maybe even today. No later than tomorrow. We have to make plans.'

'We think you should leave town, Mr Cole.'

It was the newspaper man who blurted out the reason for the confrontation.

'Leave town?' Ethan almost laughed out loud at the idea. 'You want me to leave?'

Mayor Buckle stepped forward.

'Ethan, your family have been my friends since before you were born. You've lived here all your life. I know what this town means to you. Surely you don't want to see it become a bloodbath? All we're asking is that you leave town for a short time. At least until these men realize there is nothing here for them.'

He paused to judge Ethan Cole's reaction. Surely this man, who had sent his nephew and the boy's mother to Union City for their own safety must realize that the rest of the town deserved the same consideration?

Ethan turned to face the young lawman.

'What do you say, Sheriff? You're the law around here.'

Jesse shuffled uncomfortably. 'I guess that would be for the best. That way Reno will see there's nothing for him here.'

Ethan tried to keep his temper under control but he could feel the anger rising.

'And if I leave town, you think that will be the end of it? Reno and his men will hunt me down, fill me full of bullets and you can all have a nice town funeral and say how sorry you all are.'

'Now hold on there, Ethan!' Mayor Buckle snapped back. 'This fight is none of our making, it's between you and this fella Reno. We have to think of the whole town and the safety of our citizens.'

'And you think that if I leave everything will be fine? Believe me, Mayor, you don't know Reno. I do and if I leave he'll come after me but once that's done, he'll be back. The message will have got out that this town isn't up to fight for itself. He will want the town — and he will have the men to take it. A man who planned to kill the president is not easily satisfied. If you don't face up to him now he will take over the town and your lives. Reno has failed in what he set out to do — write himself into the nation's history books.'

Ethan noticed that the newspaper-man was scribbling down every word while the mayor stood silently by and Lassiter shuffled nervously from foot to foot.

'It won't matter whether I'm here, you have to stand up to him, Sheriff,' Ethan said turning to Lassiter. 'The bank robbery was just the start. A message. Unless you face up to Reno there'll be blood on the streets of Clarkston and if you run me out none of it will be mine. I could be long gone and out of the state before Reno and his men ride in. But that will only make him madder than a rabid coyote. And if he's got that mad Irishman Rafferty and an ice-cool Texan name of Dillon riding with him, Reno will take this town apart.'

He turned and headed back towards the house but he was stopped in his tracks when Mayor Buckle called after him.

'Hold it there, Ethan. Maybe we were being a bit hasty. If you reckon that Reno and his men will come whether you stay or go, maybe it's better if you're here when he comes. Sounds like Jesse here's gonna need all the help and guns he can get.'

Ethan turned slowly, studied the trio and looked beyond them at the town that had been his home all his life. Was he speaking the truth? Or was he gambling with the lives of people who had been friends of his family for as long as he could remember?

But Daniel Reno had also been his friend. He owed his life to the proud, aristocratic soldier who had tried to save his younger brother's life at the

Battle of Five Forks and the two men were locked as comrades in the Confederate cause. But all that had changed. From the moment Ethan had learned of the true reason behind the raid on the train, all friendship and loyalty, feelings of obligation and gratitude had vanished, Daniel Reno was now the enemy. And he was a madman.

'Then I guess we ought to make plans,' he said at last. 'We have to be ready for whenever he comes.'

*   *   *

Jesse Lassiter shrugged his shoulders as he left the bar room and headed for his next call. Men's outfitter Finn Anderson was the first to turn him down in his quest to recruit and arm deputies.

Anderson flicked the ash off the end of his cigar and took another sip of his early morning drink.

'Sorry, Jesse, I'm no gunman. I like Ethan. He's one of my customers as well as a friend but it's his fight and I can't be involved. I reckon you should persuade him to leave town till the whole thing blows over.'

The rest of the calls had produced similar results.

Charlie Black, who had moved in at the end of the war to manage the stage depot on the fringe of town, told Jesse, 'It ain't my fight, Sheriff. I hardly know this man Cole except that he's a storekeeper, so, no, you can't count on me.'

It was the same at the doc's and the undertaker's and retired sheriff Ben Dawson was cool on the idea of taking up his guns again.

'Sorry, Jesse. I like Ethan, but you're wearing the badge now. I just want to put my feet up and watch the world go by. I've done my time.'

Brad Lake had regularly boasted of his talents as a sharpshooter but Jesse knew that they were more about fairground trick shots and beer bottles on fences and his enthusiasm vanished when Jesse told him that he was the only man who had agreed to become a deputy.

'Whoa there, Jesse. Get yourself a few more men and I'll join you. But you and me against a bunch of hired killers? That ain't for me, friend.'

The rest of the men he visited pointed out their responsibilities as husbands and fathers and as Jesse walked back to his office he knew that it would be Ethan and himself against Reno's men. And it was not a fight he was relishing.

He was deep in thought as he pushed open his office door and was about to slump into his chair when he realized that he had a visitor.

'Reverend? What can I do for you?' Jesse threw his gunbelt on to his desk and walked over to the coffee pot that was a permanent fixture in the office.

The clergyman got to his feet. Joshua Tullett was an imposing figure, broad-shouldered, several inches taller than the sheriff.

'The mayor tells me you've spoken to Ethan Cole and he is refusing to leave town.'

Jesse nodded. 'He says he's staying and there's nothing we can do.'

The clergyman grunted.

'Maybe,' he said thoughtfully. 'Then you will have to arrest him.'

Jesse laughed without humour. 'Arrest Ethan Cole. For what?'

'Breaking some town ordinance. You could think of something.'

Jesse placed his coffee mug on the desk and stared at the man in black but before he could speak Tullett hurried on: 'Sheriff, you know my position. I have to consider my congregation. Mr Cole believes the situation is serious enough for him to have his nephew and the boy's mother taken to the safety of Union City yet doesn't consider his fellow citizens important enough to include their safety in his plans.'

He paused but Jesse realized that the pompous speech was not over.

'I do not wish to undermine your

217

authority but I strongly suggest that you take Cole into custody and, if necessary, remove him from the town by force.'

Jesse Lassiter had been sheriff of Clarkston for barely a month — almost all of that on trial, but in the last twenty-four hours he had started to wonder if this was the job for him. First the mayor, then that newspaperman and now this domineering clergyman were all trying to tell him what to do.

'And when Reno and his men arrive, what then? Do I escort them to where I leave Ethan Cole? Are you crazy?'

Joshua Tullett blustered. 'I merely thought that if Cole was escorted to another nearby town and kept in custody until Reno and his gang move on, wouldn't that be a solution to our problems?'

'By passing them on to somebody else who has no part in this? No, sir. I suggest you stick with your goodwill to all men and fire and brimstone preachings that your congregation like so much and leave the real world to those of us who have to live in it.'

Tullett retrieved his black wide-brimmed hat from the table and pushed his way past the young man wearing the badge, heading for the door. Before leaving he turned to make one last warning:

'Let's hope we don't live to regret this day, Sheriff,' he said and left the office.

The street was deserted when Tullett stepped out into the sunlight. He had failed to persuade the sheriff to do what was right. Ethan Cole wasn't the only man in Clarkston who had reason to fear the arrival of a group of gunmen.

Joshua Tullett had been on the run for too long. And, if what he had heard about Daniel Reno and his associates was correct, that was about to end. Among those riding in alongside the Confederate major would be the man who had threatened to gun him down the next time they met: mad Irishman Martin Rafferty.

When Zeke Chisholm came to the decision that he would like to spend the rest of his days in some quiet backwater town he knew that there would be little chance to add to the wealth he had amassed and squandered over the years.

And Chisholm liked money.

But he knew that time, and maybe luck, was running out. It was time to hang up his guns, his spurs and everything else that went with his life outside the law. He had been on the run too long.

Chisholm liked the idea of a change of lifestyle. And what better way to do it than move from outlaw to clergyman with nothing more than a change of clothing? And a change of name. Zeke Chisholm was no name for a minister. Joshua, now that was a good Biblical name. He would be a Joshua. And Tullett, that was the name of the drunken cowhand he had gunned down up in Kansas a few years back.

The Reverend Joshua Tullett — that was how he would announce himself.

But before that there was the matter of one last job before he settled into his quiet life. And the man he turned to was his hard-drinking friend Martin Rafferty. Together the pair had raided many a bank before drinking, whoring and gambling away the loot until the next time.

The war was of little interest to Chisholm and, as an Irishman, Rafferty wasn't able to decide which side deserved his support.

It was not until two years into the conflict that Martin suddenly announced that he had been persuaded by a Major Reno to throw in his lot with the Confederacy. The pay, Reno had convinced him, was better. And Martin had been happy with that.

'The blue coats remind me too much of the bloody English and you know I can't stand those arrogant bastards telling everybody how to live their lives. No offence, my friend, I know your mother comes from the old country.'

'No offence taken,' Chisholm had told him. He had no love for the English; or the North, the South, or anybody else. Money and what it meant was where his loyalties lay.

It was their last job together that now haunted the bogus clergyman as he strode down the silent main street towards the Coles' house. He remembered the night he had run out on Rafferty while the Irishman snored off the effects of his latest binge. Chisholm had emptied his friend's saddle-bag of the Irishman's share of the loot they had taken from the bank and headed out of the territory.

A few weeks later, Bible in hand and dressed all in the sombre black of a man of the cloth, he had ridden his buggy into Clarkston and introduced himself as the town's new parson of the parish.

Three years after his arrival he was established in the church as a pillar of a small South Tennessee town. But all that was about to change.

His past was about to catch up with him.

An hour later Zeke Chisholm, alias Joshua Tullett, packed his carpet bag and a heavy trunk, loaded up his buggy and headed out of Clarkston. It would be the last and biggest mistake he would ever make.

*   *   *

Ethan Cole felt calm. Three, maybe four gunmen led by his one-time friend were coming to Clarkston to kill him. He had no doubt about that, he did not need a written letter to confirm his suspicions. Daniel Reno knew exactly where to find him; he had already sent Frank Mason and the other hired guns to hunt him down. Now he would be coming himself. With more guns.

Yet Ethan still felt calm. Jesse Lassiter was young but he was honest and, from what Ethan had learned, a popular sheriff. He would have no trouble recruiting enough deputies to see off Reno's threat.

Alice and Jonathan would be well on their way to the safety of her sister's house in Union City alongside Dutch's widow so that was one major worry off his mind.

But he was still puzzled about that preacher man. Why was he so eager to persuade Ethan to leave the town where he was born and raised and had lived all his life? All that talk about serving the interest of his parishioners, thinking of the greater good and the safety of the town — how much of that was the genuine belief of the man in black?

And why had he become so jittery when Ethan repeated what he had already told the sheriff and the mayor, that Reno would not be satisfied with finishing one job? That he would want the town — and he would take it.

Tullett had suddenly lost all pretence that his visit was a mission to talk Ethan into leaving town for the good of the people. Instead, he hastily left the house and Ethan stood on the porch steps and watched him dash off towards the church at the far end of town.

Now he was alone with his thoughts and, ironically, those thoughts included memories of happier days in the company of Daniel Reno. Even in the heat of battles where they were not expected to survive, Daniel always looked on the bright side and they had come through everything the North could throw at them until . . . that grey afternoon when death stalked the fields.

Matthew had been caught in some heavy crossfire. His horse had been shot from beneath him and he was scrambling through the thickening smoke when the bullet came, hitting him full in the back. Daniel had been the first to his aid, trying desperately to pull him to the safety of a nearby trench, kneeling over him when Ethan appeared out of the gloom.

Matthew had died in his brother's arms. It was as though the entire war, the guns, the cannons, the screams, had all been silenced as a mark of respect for the death of a young soldier.

When Matthew had breathed his last the sounds of mayhem returned. Together Daniel and Ethan had carried the lifeless young body out of the field of battle and from there to a place where he could receive a Christian burial. Ethan could never forget that Daniel Reno. But this one, the man who had plotted the assassination of the president, the man who was on his way to Clarkston to kill him? This Daniel Reno was a stranger and by the end of the day one or both of them would be lying dead in a dusty street of small town Tennessee.

★   ★   ★

Joshua Tullett's hopes of a quiet, unnoticed escape from Clarkston and the guns of a man he had betrayed were shattered when the four horsemen appeared from around the bend and blocked his way forward.

226

They were almost on top of him before he had any chance to take evasive action. The road was narrow, not wide enough even for a single horseman to pass a buggy, and they came around the sharp, concealed bend at little more than a trot, clearly in no hurry to reach where they were heading.

Panic seized the man in black as he took in the familiar figure at the edge of the line, riding slightly distant from the others. Red-faced, as he always knew him, his features roughened by a three-day growth of red beard and his wellworn clothes dust-covered, the man was exactly as he remembered.

The approaching riders reined their mounts to a halt, completely blocking the only route out of Clarkston to Knoxville in the north. All four leaned forward in their saddles and Tullett was forced to pull his buggy to a halt. There was no way to pass.

It was the man on the right edge of the four-man line who moved forward.

'Well, bejasus, would you believe it?' Rafferty's Irish brogue became more pronounced whenever he thought the occasion needed it, or whenever he had an audience. 'If it isn't my old long lost friend all dressed up like a man of the church, to be sure. And how are you this fine morning, Zeke Chisholm?'

The tone was mocking and the derision was not lost on Tullett.

'Good morning, Martin,' he said feebly. 'Are you all heading for Clarkston?'

'To be sure, now what other town is there along this road, Zeke, my boy?' He turned in his saddle and faced the others. 'Major, I'd like you to say hello to my friend Zeke Chisholm. And you Tex. You say hello, too. And you Regan. You say hello to my old friend.'

Tullett felt the tension mounting inside him. Or was it fear? He had hoped to be well clear of the town when Reno, Rafferty and the other bank robbers arrived. But now he was face to face with his worst fear — the man he had deserted and robbed of almost $5,000. He was staring into the face of the man who was smiling down at him.

The Irishman climbed down from his saddle and walked slowly towards the rig. 'So how have you been, Zeke? You never got chance to say a proper goodbye.'

Tullett felt cornered. 'Look, Marty, I — '

'Ah, now, Zeke my boy, you don't have to explain anything to me. I know all about it. But my friends here, now they would like to hear what happened. Why you suddenly decided we were no longer partners and why you decided to ride out in the middle of the night after you had emptied my saddle-bag of . . . what was it now . . . five thousand dollars? Go on, you tell 'em. Five thousand. Now that buys a lotta whiskey and a lotta women, wouldn't you say?'

Tullett looked at the faces of the three men still sitting motionless in their saddles. In the middle was a stout, grey-haired man with a look of authority. Rafferty called him major so he must be Reno, the man who was gunning for Ethan Cole. Next to him was a thin, sour-face critter with a drooping moustache, dark, deep-set eyes and a long, straight nose. He looked as though he feared that his face would crack into pieces if he allowed himself a smile.

The fourth member of the quartet, broader and more solidly built than the others, appeared unmoved by the whole scene. He simply sat and stared.

'What's wrong, Zeke? Something gotten hold of your tongue?'

Before Tullett could think of anything to say in his defence the Irishman badgered him further.

'Y'know, Zeke, it's funny how things turn out. There's you, all dressed up like you are on the way to a family funeral while here's me, your old Irish pal and partner flat broke without a new pair of pants to call my own. Here we are meeting up after all this time and — '

'Listen, Marty — ' Tullett began, but before he could get in another word, Rafferty had drawn his six-gun and was holding it menacingly under his old partner's nose.

'I ain't quite finished yet, old friend,' he sneered. 'You see, meeting you here might just be the change of luck I need. I think we can both agree on something, don't you?'

Puzzled, the fake preacher waited for what was coming. Rafferty re-holstered his gun, leaned up and dragged the other man from the rig.

'You owe me, Zeke and I aim to collect here and now. How much of my five thousand you still got? Three? Two, maybe?'

Tullett didn't answer. Instead he looked over the shoulder of his tormentor at the three men still mounted. But if he was hoping to see some sign of possible rescue he was out of luck.

The man with the drooping moustache snarled: 'Get on with what you're planning, Irish. We ain't got all day.'

Rafferty pulled the frightened man closer so that only a few inches separated their faces. 'Hear that, Zeke? My friends are getting impatient. Thing is, are you worth risking a hanging for? I mean, there's nobody here, no witnesses, just my friends and they, well they've got other things on their mind.'

Tullett was almost choking on his fear. The bravado that had been part of his life when he rode with outlaw gangs had long since deserted him. He was alone. 'You . . . you ain't gonna shoot me, Marty. We've been partners.'

Rafferty pushed him away and sneered.

'To be sure, I remember. I think you're the one who forgot that. So you can count this as your lucky day. I'll settle for what money you've got in those bags there. I should put you down like the lying cheating dog you are but

I'm feeling generous. Just empty those bags and fill my saddlebag over there and you can be on your way.'

Hurriedly, Tullett did as he was ordered, fumbling frantically with the bundles of notes, many of them he had pilfered from the church and the town, and stuffing them into Rafferty's saddle-bag.

Without another word he climbed back aboard his rig, slapped his reins across the horse's rear and nodded his relief and gratitude at the Irishman.

He was about to turn out of sight when Rafferty, halfway through re-mounting suddenly stopped.

'You know something, you guys, I reckon I don't feel so generous after all.'

He reached for the sheath strapped to his saddle, withdrew his Springfield and, taking careful aim, fired a bullet into the back of Joshua Tullett. The man in black stiffened and then slumped to his left.

Rafferty slid the rifle back into its

sleeve and re-mounted.

'Never did like him,' he said, digging his heels into the horse.

The killing had started.

12

James Kerring was alone in his office, studying the next front page of the *Clarkston Informer*. He was pleased with his handiwork and allowed himself a smile of self-satisfaction. Of course, the events reported on his front page had not yet happened and the newspaper would not appear until the time was right.

But he was working in advance of the fateful day that he knew lay ahead. ETHAN COLE SHOT DEAD IN GUN BATTLE was the headline he had scribbled on his note pad and the one he would eventually use to record the coming shoot-out.

He read through the report that would soon be appearing below the banner headline.

Ethan Cole, Clarkston storekeeper and former soldier, died on the main street of the town where he had lived all his life, gunned down by an old friend and three other men who came to town for revenge.

While there are many in town who will mourn the death of a valued friend and member of the community the question has to be asked: Did Ethan Cole's stubbornness cost him his life?

The Informer knows that he was well aware of the impending danger and he even explained it to the sheriff and members of the town council. But when asked to leave town for the safety and security of others he flatly refused, even though he had already sent his young nephew and the boy's mother to a safe retreat in Union City.

The Informer feels it our duty to ask why he did not show the townspeople whom he had lived amongst all his life the same consideration. *This newspaper may find itself unpopular for asking uncomfortable questions but it is our duty, as our name suggests, to inform the people of Southern Tennessee of events that concern them.*

Ethan Cole was a popular man but we must ask: Was that popularity deserved? He did admit to being a member of a group of Confederate soldiers who planned to rob a train carrying the President of the United States and only at the last moment did he turn on his co-conspirators, an action that brought death to our streets on a quiet sunny morning. Was that how a respected soldier should behave?

Kerring threw down his pen and leaned back in his seat. The rest of the report — the actual shooting — would be an eye-witness account, viewed from the safety of his upstairs room at the Clarkston Hotel.

Kerring had been in the newspaper business for long enough to know that his views might upset many of his readers, but they could not ignore them. He was writing nothing that was untrue and if Cole's death aroused their passion he would have achieved what he intended.

With that in mind, he slid open his desk drawer and poured himself a large slug of whiskey.

★　★　★

Henry Buckle slumped over his desk with the air of a man who had the troubles of the world on his shoulders. The mayor of Clarkston was indeed a worried man. The woman at his side, a buxom redhead whose generous charms he regarded among the fringe benefits of his status as the town's leading citizen, massaged his shoulders trying to offer some grains of comfort in his hour of need.

But, for once, Mayor Buckle found

no solace in the fingers of saloon singer Kitty Furness. Even her soothing words, 'Nobody will blame you, sweetheart,' offered no consolation and he removed her hands from his shoulders and rose from his seat.

What was wrong with this stupid woman? Did she not realize he was about to lose his town?

Why was this happening to him? First there was the bank robbery, the first that Clarkston had ever known. And now there was the news that some gun-crazy rebel was riding into town to kill Ethan Cole.

Buckle liked Ethan; he had known him all his life and his father had been his closest friend in the bad years of the drought that had cost so many families their stock and their crops. But now he had to convince this best friend's son that he had to leave. If what Ethan had said was the truth, this man Reno would not be satisfied with one killing. He would be taking over the town. And it was *his* town.

The mayor stalked the room, glowering occasionally in Kitty's direction. What was he to do? How could he stop Reno and his hired guns from coming to town? Or, if that was impossible, maybe there had to be a way to prevent bloodshed, to protect his own position as Mayor of Clarkston, even to elevate himself to the position of saviour of the town.

He resumed his seat at his wide oak desk, opened a drawer, withdrew a sheet of notepaper and began frantically to write. For almost five minutes he scribbled furiously, pausing occasionally as if deliberating over the choice of word.

Eventually he finished the note, folded it neatly and placed it in an envelope. He stood up, put his arms around the woman.

'Kitty, I've got a little errand for you.'

Puzzled, the woman gave him a quizzical look.

He thrust the envelope into her hand. 'I want you to deliver this note to

Ethan Cole. And I want you to hurry.'

Still perplexed, Kitty examined the envelope. 'What is it?'

Henry smiled at her. 'Nothing for you to worry about, my dear. You leave that to me. Just deliver it to the Cole house and wait for a reply.'

'And then?'

'And then, Kitty my love, we shall know whether Ethan Cole is half the man the people of Clarkston believe he is.'

★　★　★

Jesse Lassiter threw his hat on to the table, mopped the sweat from his brow and poured himself a drink from the pitcher of water. He stared at the man busy wiping down the barrel of a rifle.

The man looked up. 'I figure from your silence you have had no luck,' he said laying the Springfield to one side.

'You figure right, Ethan. Not a single volunteer agreed to sign up as a deputy,' the young sheriff answered grimly. 'Everybody I asked said the same — this is not their fight.'

'You told them what would happen once Reno had gotten me out of his way?'

Lassiter shrugged.

'They didn't believe you?' It was what Ethan had expected. 'They thought I was stretching the truth to save my own hide.'

'Guess so. The question is, now what do we do?'

Ethan smiled. 'I don't have a choice, Sheriff. I sit here and wait. But you, well, you're a young man with a future in this town. I don't think you reckoned on this sort of situation when you took that badge and unless I'm mistaken you don't really want to be here right now. I suggest you do what everybody else here is doing. Keep off the streets until it's all over. Then, well I don't suppose I'll be around to give you any advice.'

Jesse felt the anger rising and when he spoke they were the words of an angry man.

'Yes, Ethan. You're right. I don't want to be here and like the rest of the folk here I think this is your fight and not theirs. But I'm the law in Clarkston and if I let Reno and his men ride in here and gun you down in the street then I wouldn't be doing what I'm paid for. To uphold the law.

'So I won't be hiding away until it's over. I'll be doing my job but right now I intend to keep asking around, and — ' he picked up his hat from the table and was preparing to leave when there was a loud banging on the door.

Ethan edged towards the window and eased aside the lace curtains.

'You can relax, Jesse. It's Kitty Furness, the mayor's woman,' he told the lawman who had moved into a corner and had unholstered his six-gun.

He opened the door and stepped aside to let his visitor enter the house. Ethan had seen Kitty Furness around town but had never really got to know anything about her other than she was a singer in one of Clarkston's two entertainment establishments. However, he always remembered her as a smiling, friendly customer whenever she made one of her rare visits to his store. But she wasn't smiling now. And there was nothing friendly about her appearance.

She thrust the message from Buckle into Ethan's hand.

'Henry said you might want to give me an answer,' she said curtly.

Ethan unfolded the sheet and read the message.

I am making this final appeal to you as a neighbour and a friend to help prevent bloodshed on the streets of Clarkston. If what you say is true and that this Major Reno will not be satisfied until he has taken over the town, then that is something we as citizens will have to endure. We will still have the opportunity to leave if we wish. However, you may be wrong. It is highly possible that Reno has no designs on our town and is merely out to gain revenge on the man who betrayed him. You, Ethan.

If you were to leave town before Reno and his men arrived I am sure your secret, that you were initially part of a plot to assassinate the President of the United States, will go with you to your grave. But who knows what will happen if you stay? Would you wish your part in that plot to be relayed to your nephew Jonathan?

I am not the only person in town who has noticed how sweet you are on your brother's widow and how fond you are of the boy. Surely you would not wish him to grow up with the knowledge that his favourite uncle was, I won't use polite words here, a traitor. And how would his mother feel about that? I cannot promise that your past will remain a secret even after your death if you persist in this folly of putting other lives at risk.

I leave you to your conscience but time is short. Believe me, Ethan, even if you survive this unnecessary gunplay you will be left friendless here in Clarkston. And I urge you again to think of the dishonour it will bring to your family. Do the right thing by everybody and leave town before it is too late.

Mayor H. Buckle

Ethan finished reading the note and stuffed it into his shirt. What should he do? If he stayed he had no doubt that Buckle would release what he knew to that newspaperman who owned the *Informer* and that Jonathan and Alice would be faced with an unbearable truth. He couldn't let that happen.

'Seems like you won't have to recruit any guns after all, Sheriff.'

He turned to face Kitty. 'Tell the mayor that I have got his message and I will do as he says.' She turned to leave but Ethan reached out and clasped her arm. 'You can also tell him that if he ever breathes a word of what is in this note I'll return to Clarkston. To kill him.'

★   ★   ★

The pain was excruciating and the man in the rig wanted to scream out in his agony. But that would have been suicide. Instead, he lay still, his only hope if he wished to cling on to life. And Zeke Chisholm (alias Joshua Tullett) still loved life. He had grown used to being a respected preacher, the cloth of the clergy becoming the perfect cloak to hide his lawless past.

Now the past had caught up with him. Martin Rafferty, his friend from days gone by, had robbed him of everything, put a bullet in his back and left him for dead.

Despite the fierceness of the pain he managed to listen and wait. Eventually, the sound he had been praying to hear, finally reached his ears: they were riding off. He could vaguely make out the Irishman's chuckle but as it faded he struggled into a sitting position.

But what now? He did not know the territory so the next town could be as much as a day's ride away and he needed a doctor. Without help he would be dead before nightfall and Rafferty would have won.

Somehow he had to get back to Clarkston. He had no notion of how much blood he was losing or how close the bullet was to his vital organs but if he stayed where he was he would surely bleed to death in a few hours.

Gripping the reins in his left hand, he needed all his strength to swing the rig around and head it back to town. The ruts in the track caused him to wince at the stabbing pains and twice he slumped forward almost losing the will to carry on. But somehow he managed to keep the rig on the road and slowly the horse dragged him in the direction of Clarkston.

Henry Buckle was feeling pleased with himself. Kitty had returned with the message from Ethan Cole and he stood at his window and watched in anticipation. The Cole house was in direct view with his own office and twice he saw Ethan come out first to saddle his horse and then to load his blanket and saddlebags.

He was preparing to leave.

Henry smiled and turned to the other man in the room.

'I know it's early but this calls for a drink, Silas.'

The bank owner was still suffering from the pain of the injuries sustained in the robbery but managed to return the smile.

Buckle opened the oak cabinet with its array of expensive Irish crystal and withdrew two of the carved drinking glasses from his collection.

'You know, Silas, my friend, I have the feeling that all will turn out well for both of us.'

The bank man accepted the whiskey and his puzzled frown encouraged the mayor to continue.

'Look at it like this. I have managed to save the town from becoming the scene of a bloody gunfight and you have survived a brutal attack and robbery. The people of Clarkston will be grateful to me and sympathetic to you. What more could we ask? Here's to your good health, my friend.'

The bank man raised his glass in acknowledgement but the frown never left his pale, thin face.

'You are assuming, Henry that these ... these gunmen ... killers ... who are looking for Ethan will not bother us after all.'

'Why should they? Cole will no longer be here. He is the man they want. All that talk about taking over the town, that was all so much nonsense from a man desperate to redeem himself in the eyes of the whole town. Believe me, Silas, when Reno and his men find that Ethan has left town they will chase after him and we will never see them again. Trust me.'

Silas Jones sipped his whiskey but said nothing. He had his doubts. Ethan Cole was not a man for fanciful exaggeration and if Reno and that man who had said he was from the railroad company were behind the bank robbery, what was to stop them returning and carrying out what Ethan had predicted?

He finished his drink and rose from his seat. He refused a refill on the pretext that he should look in at the bank and he headed for the door. He was reaching for the handle when he looked out of the office window and suddenly froze.

'Henry! Henry, look!'

Mayor Buckle emptied his glass and hurried across the room.

'Isn't that . . . ?' Silas stammered.

The mayor pulled open the door and stepped out on to the boardwalk.

'My God!' he shouted. 'It's Tullett . . . and it looks like he's been shot.'

* ★ ★

Reno looked across at the three men he had hired to carry out his work. How much longer would he need them at his side? Once he had rid himself of that traitor Cole and the town was in his hands what use would they be to him? Sure he had promised them a share of the rich pickings, but hired guns were ten-a-dollar now that the war was over and the display of viciousness by the Irishman that morning had confirmed Reno's belief that he was unstable.

The Texan Dillon was different. He said little but Reno suspected he kept many thoughts to himself. He could be a dangerous man to cross. Perhaps keeping him around would be wisest.

As for Regan, he was nothing more than hired help. True, he had done a good job posing as the railroad executive and setting up the robbery, but that would be the limit of his usefulness: he could be replaced at any time.

But that was all for the future. Right now he needed their support for at least one more hour. Getting to his feet, the urge towards more power surging through his blood, Reno stood over the trio who were crouched idly cursing their hands in their latest time-killing card game.

'Right, men. It is time to go into Clarkston and do what we are here to do,' Reno said quietly. 'In two hours the town will be ours.'

Rafferty jumped up, threw away his cards and laughed like an excited schoolboy.

'Now that's what we've been waiting to hear, major. A town of whiskey and women waiting just for us.' He cackled a throaty, humourless laugh.

Nobody else smiled. Dillon moved silently away to saddle up his horse, Regan spat out the remainder of his tobacco and Reno tried to hide his disgust.

This was a man he had only recently saved from a jail sentence — not for the

253

first time — and who was now treating this mission like a raid on a whorehouse. Reno decided that Martin Rafferty, was, just like Ethan, a dead man walking.

★ ★ ★

'Get him inside and be careful. He may have lost a lot of blood.'

Doc Callaway's voice was scarcely above a whisper as he fussed around the unconscious figure of Joshua Tullett. It was as though he was afraid of rousing the clergyman. Henry Buckle and Jesse Lassiter carried Tullett inside the sheriff's office while the doctor swept the desk top clear to provide an improvised table. The two men lowered Tullett on to the desk, face down and moved away.

When Buckle spoke to the sheriff there was fear in his voice.

'Has Cole left town yet?' he asked.

'I saw him earlier,' Lassiter told him. 'Said he had some business to attend to before he rode out.'

'Business? What business can he still have here, for God's sake?' Buckle snapped. 'He should be long gone by now.'

'He still has the store, Mayor,' Jesse answered. 'He'll be making sure it's all secure for when Jonathan and his ma come home. It'll be theirs now, and — '

'Cut the happy family shit, Jesse. Get out there and make sure he's gone before those bastards who — who did that,' he gestured towards the desk, 'before they get into town.'

'You reckon that's the work of this man Reno?'

'Who else?'

Suddenly there was the sound of coughing and spluttering from the man on the desk. Buckle watched as the doctor leaned closely to his patient, as if trying to hear something the man was trying to say. The mayor waited impatiently for Callaway to relay any message.

Eventually, the medical man straightened up. 'Four men. And they're coming here,' he said. 'Those were his last words.'

★   ★   ★

The sun was high in a clear sky and beat down with a savage heat when the first gunshot was heard.

It was three minutes after noon.

Ethan had reached the small white church with its smart fence and neatly maintained cemetery when he spotted the four riders. They were too far in the distance to distinguish but Ethan had no doubt about the identity of the man on the right of the group sitting tall in the saddle, a man of authority. Confederate Major Daniel Reno had arrived.

The rifle bullet scattered the dust a dozen or so yards away from Ethan's feet. It was a signal shot, not aimed at killing or injuring. It was fired as a warning.

Ethan dismounted, withdrew his own rifle from its sheath then slapped the rump of his horse to send it trotting away. It was too late to run now. It was time to stand and fight for his life and he was a man alone. Behind him the main street of Clarkston was deserted, the town's inhabitants hiding behind their curtains, dreading the worst but unwilling to stand and face the four killers now approaching the outskirts of their quiet Tennessee homes.

Ethan realized that, exposed as he was, he had no chance against Reno and his men. Whether they liked it or not, the citizens of Clarkston were about to be reluctant guests at a shoot-out that would end in death on their streets.

Scouring the surrounding area, Ethan ran for the cover of a disused livery stable which he knew opened out on to a back alley that led to the rear of the sheriff's office and jail-house.

He figured it would be ten, maybe twelve minutes, before Reno arrived in town, enough time for him to pick out a vantage point offering the best chance to defend himself. Reno would be in no hurry. He would be enjoying this; the idea of having his prey running for cover would appeal to his sense of power.

Ethan re-checked his six-guns, both fully loaded, and his rifle, and hurried along the alley. Despite the midday hour, there was an eerie silence about the town, as though the world was waiting for something evil to happen. He could almost touch the fear.

Maybe it was not too late to round up his horse and ride out, forcing Reno to chase him. At least the town would be safe — for a short time. But if he was made to pursue Ethan, Reno would hunt him down and eventually return vengeful and full of anger. And the town would pay.

No, Ethan told himself, now was the time and the place to settle this.

He was still thinking about his options when he arrived at the rear of the Clarkston Hotel. A wooden stair-case led up from the alley to the top floor and Ethan's memory served him well enough to remind him that the main rooms at the side had a balcony overlooking the main street. From there, he would be able to see them before they caught sight of him.

It was a small advantage but with the odds of four guns to one against him he needed all the help he could muster.

Slipping through the rear entrance and into the hotel kitchen, he looked around for any possible escape route but knew instantly that if he needed to negotiate a way out, the chances were that it would be all over.

Beyond the kitchen was the hotel's reception area, unmanned as he had expected but he was about to climb the circular staircase when his attention was drawn to a shuffling sound beyond the desk. Firmly gripping his rifle he edged towards the source of the noise. He paused in mid-stride. Was it possible that Reno had sent a man on ahead? Ethan thought that was unlikely — his old major would assume that a stranger would not go unnoticed in Clarkston.

But there was no profit in taking chances.

Raising his rifle, he snapped out his order: 'Come on out and make it slow. Hands first, out in front of you.'

Nothing happened. Then: 'Don't shoot, Mr Cole. I don't mean no harm. Honest.'

A boy's voice. Young. Unbroken.

Ethan relaxed as the young figure emerged from his hiding place.

'Jason! What in blazes are you doing here?' Ethan recognized the boy as a friend of his nephew Jonathan, Jason Callaway, young son of the town's doctor.

'I — I'm sorry, I was just — ' the boy was sobbing.

'Take it easy, son.' Ethan put his arm around the boy's shoulders and waited for an explanation.

'Pa's in the sheriff's office next door and the reverend was hurt bad and they were talking of him being shot an' all and the killers coming to town an' I wanted to see what a killer looks like so

I hid in here because I thought it was safe and when I heard that Pa needed to go to see old Locker the undertaker I knew I had to hide because if he knew I was here he — '

It was all delivered without a pause for breath and the boy was only silenced when Ethan placed his hand across the youngster's mouth.

'Easy, Jason. I reckon you should head home before your pa finds out what you've been doing following him around like that.'

'You won't tell him, Mr Cole?'

Ethan smiled. Jason Callaway was the same age as his nephew, now safely hiding away, and unlike his friend, well out of harm's way.

A freckle-faced goofy sort of kid, Jason was his nephew's closest friend and, Ethan believed, a good kid.

'I won't tell him, Jason, I promise. Now run along before he sticks his head out of the sheriff's office and sees you.'

The boy ran his shirt-sleeved arm

across his nose, wiped his tears and headed for the door. But as he reached the exit he stopped in his tracks and turned.

'Mr Cole?'

'Yes, Jason? What is it?'

'I — I sure hope those men don't kill you, too.'

He ran out of the hotel.

★   ★   ★

Jesse's mind was in turmoil. Mayor Buckle and the rest of the town had deserted Ethan Cole and he had gone along with them for his own selfish reasons.

But he was the sheriff; he had been appointed to uphold the law in Clarkston and one of its leading citizens was under threat from a group of killers. Yet he had left Ethan to stand alone. And why? Not because he believed Cole did not deserve his support. It was, Jesse reluctantly conceded, because Ethan was a love rival.

The young lawman had kept his feelings for Alice Cole to himself for a long time but since her husband had been killed in the war he had been waiting for the right moment to express himself to the young widow. But he had not failed to notice how close she was with her dead husband's brother and how her young son spent hours with his uncle.

But the killing of Joshua Tullett had changed all that. This was no longer a personal choice for Jesse. He could not sit back and ignore the threat to the town. There would be no peace in Southern Tennessee if Reno's men were allowed to escape justice.

He watched in silence while the doctor finished wiping away the blood and Henry Buckle discussed the burial plans with the grim-faced undertaker Locker. Then, without a word, he took his gunbelt down from its place behind the door, checked the chambers of the six-gun and left the office.

The riders reached the outskirts of town before anybody spoke about what was to come. It was the Texan, Dillon, who posed the question.

'What makes you think that warning shot you fired ain't scared him off, Major? Him and just about everybody else in town, the way things look.'

He gestured towards the deserted main street.

Reno reined his horse to a halt. 'Cole's a traitor, not a coward. He won't run. He'll be around and he'll be waiting for us. Look upon this as a challenge.'

It was the Irishman who laughed.

'Four against one. To be sure, what sort of challenge is that? We can finish this business in less time than it takes to undress the cheapest whore.'

Reno didn't smile.

'You've always been a headstrong man, Martin, my boy. Maybe that's what I like about you. But let me tell you, Cole is no fool and this is his town. He'll appear where we least expect him. And he may have some help if they know you shot their reverend.'

'Zeke Chisholm was no preacher,' the Irishman protested. 'He was a penny crook.'

'But these people don't know that, Irish,' Regan argued. 'It's a small town and they will stick together. This ain't gonna be no Patrick's Day picnic.'

'Maybe . . . maybe not,' Reno mused. 'If I know Cole, he'll probably have already told them all about us. And they will not like what they've heard. They're farmers and traders. They are not gunmen.'

When they reached the livery stable through which Ethan had bolted following the warning shot, the four men dismounted. Reno had discarded his civilian clothes for this one final appearance in his army grey. He straightened his coat, checked his hat and brushed some of the dust from his uniform.

He was now ready for the last act of his military career before settling into civilian life.

'Remember, gentlemen, Cole could be hiding behind any one of these windows ready to shoot. We must spread ourselves, use the cover of the boardwalks, draw him out.' Suddenly he stopped speaking and pointed down the main street. 'Seems like we are expected.'

Rafferty followed the direction of the major's outstretched arm and emitted a throaty laugh. 'Some reception committee. One kid,' he mocked.

Jesse Lassiter was walking slowly towards them.

★ ★ ★

Ethan had taken the best vantage point he could find on the balcony at the side of the Clarkston Hotel when he spotted the sheriff walking slowly and nervously down the middle of the street.

What was he doing, putting himself

at risk? What did he hope to achieve? Ethan was tempted to shout out to him but that could prove fatal. A turn of the head by Lassiter would have revealed his position and he could not let that happen.

Further down the street, Mayor Henry Buckle, Silas Jones and Doc Callaway watched from the safety of a locked and barred office. Newspaperman Lerring's bravado had deserted him and he was among the daytime drinkers in the saloon who tried to ignore it all by ordering more whiskey, while across the street the good time girls at Martha's Music Hall gathered on their veranda.

At the end of the street Reno and his men waited for the approaching sheriff. He could guess what was about to happen. The lawman would warn him and his men that there was nothing in Clarkston for them, he might even try to persuade them that Cole had left town.

The boy looked unsure of himself,

not convinced that the badge he was wearing offered him any protection. He reminded Reno of many of the young men under his command during the war. Too young to fight; too young to die. But now none of that was his problem.

He stepped forward in a show of authority.

'Good day to you, Sheriff. Major Daniel Reno at your service.'

'I know who you are, Mr Reno,' he ignored the uniform. 'I'm Jesse Lassiter. I'm the sheriff here in Clarkston.'

'Who'd have guessed?' Rafferty sneered.

'I'm here to ask you to surrender your sidearms before you come into town,' Jesse said.

'May I ask why?' Daniel Reno offered a look of innocence, assuming his favourite role as sophisticated gentleman.

'There's been one killing and we don't want another.'

'And you think we are responsible for this killing?'

'I may be young, Mr Reno, but I'm not dumb. Joshua Tullett told us what happened.'

'And who is Joshua Tullett, may I ask?'

'Was,' Jesse stared coldly at the man in the grey uniform. 'He's dead. Shot in the back outside of town. He lived just long enough to tell us that there were four of them.'

'And your conclusion is that, as there are four of us, we must be responsible.'

'Are you?'

Suddenly the air of forced, false politeness vanished when Rafferty, who had been standing alongside Reno, stepped in front of the major.

'Let's cut this shit talk, Sheriff. Tullett was a double-dealing crook who deserved what he got. Sure, I was the one who killed the bastard. And you know why we're here so I suggest you go back and tell Cole to come out and face us. You can just step aside and let us get on with our business. That way nobody except Cole need get hurt.

How's that sound to you?'

Jesse knew he had to stand his ground if he was ever to mean anything as a lawman. He was sure that his knees were shaking and he knew that if he stepped aside now it would probably save his life. But what was the price he would have to pay for the rest of that life?

'Like I've said, give me your guns and you can go into town.'

The Irishman made a move for his six-gun but Reno gripped his wrist.

'Tell me, Sheriff. Has Ethan Cole surrendered his weapons? If he has not then there is at least one man in Clarkston who is armed. Why are we being denied the same?'

Jesse stiffened and Reno noticed.

'So you see, Sheriff, er, Jesse,' Reno continued, 'You cannot have one law for your friend Ethan Cole and one for everybody else in town. So why don't you just step aside and let us go about our business.'

He had hardly finished speaking

when the gunshot came. Jesse screamed in excruciating pain, clutched his thigh and crashed to the ground.

'We're through talking,' Dillon said re-holstering his gun. 'Let's do what we came to do.'

Reno looked down at the sheriff as he rolled in raging suffering.

'When it's over, I'll send the doctor,' Reno said quietly, leaning down to relieve Jesse of his gun.

Then the four men stepped out on to the main street and set out to kill Ethan Cole.

13

Ethan heard the single gunshot and feared the worst. Young Jesse had been shot, probably killed by Reno or one of his men. The wait was over; they were now coming for him.

The heat was getting to him and he removed his hat to wipe away the rivulets of sweat trickling down his forehead. His palms were moist as he gripped the butt of his rifle. He thought of Alice and Jonathan, and his dead brother killed in battle, dying in his arms. He remembered how Major Reno, then his friend as well as his officer, had tried to drag the younger Cole to safety as Ethan had scrambled through the gathering clouds of gunsmoke.

He was still remembering all this when he spotted them. They were walking slowly and had spread across the street; Dillon on the far boardwalk, the Irishman next to him, gun at the ready and his head moving swiftly from side to side as he searched out his prey. Closest to him was a big round man Ethan had never seen before. That left only Reno, and his guess was that his old commander was out of sight on the boardwalk beneath him.

Cocking his rifle, Ethan stepped forward and took aim. It was their lives or his — no time for honour and an even chance. He fired.

Dillon and Ratcliffe spun round as the big man grabbed his throat and cartwheeled into the dust, spluttering and jerking as he breathed his last.

Ethan fired again; this time the bullet ripped through a wooden post and the Texan was able to dive for safety.

The Irishman fired in the direction of the shooting but he was too hasty and the bullet flew harmlessly wide of its target.

Crouching, Ethan raced along the balcony, fired another shot more in hope than judgement, and leapt across the narrow gap that separated the hotel from its nearest neighbour, the newspaper office. Another bullet ripped through the woodwork near his shoulder but he managed to reach the safety of the cover offered by the large hoarding that announced the name, THE CLARKSTON AND SOUTH TENNESSEE INFORMER. There was still no sighting of Daniel Reno but Ethan knew he would be close at hand.

More gunfire followed but did no damage other than to spray splinters across the roof of the newspaper building.

'Show yourself, Cole. You yellow-livered coward.'

The screaming challenge came from the Irishman and Ethan was grateful for it. He could now place at least one of the would-be killers — outside the gunsmith's.

They were closing in on him but he had no intentions of staying around to wait for them. Sliding open an upstairs window, he slipped into the newspaper office and made his way down the staircase, past the printing press and the huge piles of paper ready to be turned into the next editions. Peering through the window he spotted Rafferty on the far side of the street. He was tempted to smash the glass and fire his rifle but the thought that Reno might be standing out of his line of sight only a few feet away was enough of a deterrent. To give himself away now would be like walking into a bullet.

Crossing the room he made his way to the rear of the building and out into the alley behind. A covered buggy, its horse tied to a rail, stood unattended at the side of Henry Buckle's house.

'Reckon you won't be needing this any time soon,' Ethan thought, surprising himself that he actually muttered the words. Releasing the horse from its tether, he coaxed the animal into a position facing the main street and climbed aboard. Gripping the reins, he eased the buggy forward until it was well clear of the house and then lashed the horse into a gallop. As he reached the corner he gave it an extra whip and dived into the back of the buggy. Straight ahead in the middle of the street, Tex Dillon blocked the way. But the horse was at full speed now and the only way it could be stopped was with a bullet. Dillon fired but there was panic in his aim as the horse continued its gallop towards him. He flung himself to the left and at the same time fired off a shot that ripped through the canopy. Inside, Ethan took aim and fired. The shot was perfect and Dillon's dive for safety was in vain. The first bullet hit him full in the chest and although he managed to twist and attempt to return the fire he crashed into the horse trough outside the saloon. Ethan fired again, this time hitting Dillon squarely in the back. He was dead before he stopped rolling.

The runaway buggy raced down the street with Rafferty and Reno firing wildly in the hope of hitting their target. At the end of the street Ethan leapt clear, rolled in the dust and raced towards a broken down barn at the east end of town. Now he would avoid any danger to innocent bystanders caught up in crossfire. He owed the people of Clarkston that much, even though they had turned their backs on him when he asked for their help.

He was a man alone. His only possible ally, Jesse Lassiter was probably lying dead at the far end of town but his own chances of survival were better than when the shooting started, the fat man and Dillon were dead, leaving only Daniel Reno and Rafferty.

The sudden change of light from the blazing sun of the street to the dimness of the inside of the old barn forced Ethan to pause and take time for his eyes to adjust. When his vision became focused he studied the interior of the place he had chosen as his battlefield. Up to his right was the hayloft, and behind, four stalls that once housed the horses belonging to drifters and gamblers on their overnight stops in

Clarkston. In one corner was a broken-down buckboard and a water butt. For the rest, it was empty except for a scurrying rabbit disturbed by his arrival.

Ethan re-loaded his rifle, checked his six-gun and settled behind the buckboard to wait. The minutes passed and he took the time to assess the options Reno would be discussing with the Irishman. Would they come rushing in, guns firing? Ethan almost chuckled at the idea. Daniel Reno had never been the type of soldier to willingly put himself at the wrong end of a gun.

Ethan tried to recall the layout around the old barn. A corral, a deserted house and a disused brewery, the east end of town had long since been abandoned by the people of Clarkston. The town's prosperity, soon to grow even stronger with the arrival of the railroad depot, was centred on the west. There was a ghostly uneasy silence as Ethan took more time to study his surroundings but it was eventually broken by the sound of a gunshot. Ethan tensed, expecting more. Instead, it was followed by the barking voice of Daniel Reno.

'You in there, Captain? Are you listening?'

Ethan didn't answer. He knew Reno wasn't expecting one. He had the stage and he was going to use it.

'You betrayed me, Ethan Cole! You deserted me! Now you've killed two of my men and I have come to collect on that debt!'

More silence.

Ethan shuffled from his crouched position towards the open-ended side of the barn.

Reno resumed his tirade against everybody he could lay his tongue to but where was Rafferty?

Suddenly, without warning, the question was answered. Reno's ranting was a diversion. From behind, Ethan heard the sound of creaking woodwork. The Irishman had climbed the rickety outside staircase that led to the hayloft without making a sound. Lack of use and care had caused the wood to rot during the harsh winters but it had been strong enough to take the Irishman's weight, until, that is, he reached the top. Then it gave way, forcing Rafferty to dive inside the barn. Ethan spun round to see the redheaded man from Donegal staring down at him, gun in hand.

'I'd really like to pull this trigger, Captain,' he smirked. 'But you know the major, he'd like to finish what he started and you are really in his bad books after you ran out on us. He's been seriously mad ever since and it's not in my interests to upset him any more. You know that.' He waved his six-gun menacingly. 'Now, throw out the rifle and move away, hands in the air.'

There was no time to think; Ethan had to act or die. Flinging himself at the only place that denied the Irishman a clear shot, he was a split second too slow.

Rafferty fired. The bullet tore into his shoulder and as he hit the ground the pain ripped through him. But he still had his gun. He aimed towards the hayloft and squeezed the trigger but as he did so, Ratcliffe flung himself to the ground, rolling over and firing blindly. The pair exchanged shots without inflicting any damage other than scattering a few more splinters.

'He said you wouldn't give up easy,' the Irishman sniggered.

Ethan felt the warm blood running down from the wound.

'The man's power crazy, Irish. The war's over.'

'Pah! Your bloody war,' Rafferty sneered. 'D'ye think I care a bloody hoot about your stupid war? North and South — you're all the same. You know, Captain, the major may be crazy that's for sure, but he's my kinda crazy. But that's not why I'm here. You ran out on us. On me. And Frank Mason. And the Dutchman. You cost us a fortune in gold and, like the major, I want to see you pay for that.'

Ethan's mind was racing. Rafferty still did not know the truth. That there was no gold, that the real reason for the raid on the train was to kill the President of the United States.

'And now you've killed Tex and the fat man. You're dangerous to leave around, Mr Cole.'

'Listen, Irish. Reno's been lyin' to you. There was no gold on that train. All Reno wanted to do was to kill Andrew Johnson, the president. He wanted to make a name for himself, like that Wilkes Booth who shot Lincoln. He wants to make himself a hero to the South and start up the war again. There was no gold.'

There was a brief silence, then: 'You're lying, Cole. You're just trying to save your skin.'

Ethan eased himself into a sitting position. The pain in his shoulder was increasing and it was clear that Rafferty was never going to be convinced. He believed everything Reno had told him.

He believed in the man who had saved him from more scrapes than he deserved and the thought that his saviour might be crazy mattered not at all.

'I guess he just didn't get round to telling you,' he said quietly as if thinking aloud.

'It looks like it's your move, Irish. We can sit here all day but I don't think that's in the major's plan.' Then he tried again: 'Has he told you what happened to Frank Mason? Did he just disappear?'

The question went unanswered but it sparked Rafferty into action. Suddenly he leapt from his hiding place behind the water butt and fired. But it was Ethan's returning shot that found the target, the bullet hitting Rafferty full in the chest. The Irishman rolled once, coughed violently and tried to raise his gun. It was a last, futile attempt to defy death. He slumped face downwards and lay still.

Ethan tried to examine the wound.

The bullet was lodged just below the shoulder blade. He had suffered worse but he had to stem the blood flow if he was to stand and face the man who had sworn to see him dead.

★ ★ ★

Outside the barn, Daniel Reno waited for the Irishman to call for him. What was keeping him? Surely he had the traitor trussed up and ready to be delivered by now. It wasn't possible that Cole had survived the surprise attack. That was inconceivable. It had been all so well planned by Reno himself. He would keep the captain occupied and the Irishman would sneak up the outside stairs and get the drop on their man. After that he would deliver him out to Reno.

It was hot and the wait was making him angry. He brushed specks of imaginary dust from his greycoat, looked around, saw that the street was still deserted and muttered, 'Cowards.'

He returned his attention to the barn.

'What's happening in there, Martin?' No reply. That worried Reno.

'Rafferty?' More silence, but that was all the confirmation the major needed.

He knew now what had happened. The Irishman had failed him.

'So, there's just you and me now, Captain Cole. I suppose that was always going to be the case. My men have all gone and your dirty little town has deserted you.'

Silence.

There was a sneer in Reno's voice when he spoke again.

'You gonna hide away all day, Captain? Or are you going to come and face me man to man?'

This time he didn't wait for an answer. Instead he hurried on, his voice rising as he began to enjoy the moment. 'I'd have thought more of you, Captain. I didn't think you were like the rest, especially that coward of a brother of yours.' He paused. 'Oh, you didn't know about that, did you? I didn't tell you. I let you think I tried to save his worthless life. Why would I? He was trying to run out on me. On you. I saw the yellow streak right down his back as he turned and fled. I don't let anybody walk out on me, Captain. Frank Mason found that out a few days ago. I didn't try to save Matthew Cole's life. I took it. I put a bullet in that stripe of yellow. It was no bluebelly who killed him, Captain. It was Daniel Reno, major in the Confederate army.'

★　★　★

Ethan sank to his knees. The pain from his shoulder was growing worse but that was not what was occupying him now. His young brother, who had died in his arms during the mayhem that was the Battle of Five Forks, had been killed not as he had been told, at the hands of the Yankees but had been gunned down, murdered, by the man who had befriended him.

He hardly heard any more as Reno stepped up his rant against Washington, the North, that coward who surrendered, Robert E. Lee, then the world in general.

Finally: 'Are you coming out to face me, Ethan? Or are you gonna rot in there with that useless Irishman you've killed? Do you know he really believed there was some gold on that train?' He roared with laughter at the memory. 'He was like a son to me, you know, Ethan. A bit like you. But then . . . sons often let you down, don't they?'

He stopped talking and started to walk towards the barn. But he halted in his tracks as Ethan appeared out of the gloom.

'I'm here, Daniel,' he said quietly.

Reno studied the man facing him. The arm hanging loose at his side, the blood running down his fingers and into the dust.

'I see Martin wasn't as bad as I painted him. He managed to get one shot into you before you killed him.'

'You shot my brother in the back,' Ethan said, unhearing. Without another word, he raised his six-gun and fired. And he fired again. And again. He emptied the gun into the twitching body of the man who had been his friend. Then he threw the empty gun aimlessly at the dead body of Major Reno and slumped to his knees.

Ethan Cole wept for the first time in his life.

Epilogue

Jonathan Cole ran down the garden path and leapt into the arms of the man who had just arrived at the gate.

The man winced and a look of alarm spread across the young boy's face.

'You hurt, Uncle?'

Ethan forced a smile and tried to shake off the reminder of his last days in Clarkston. Doc Callaway had done a good job removing the bullet from his shoulder as well as patching up Jesse Lassiter so that the young sheriff was able to hobble around with the help of a stick.

The funerals of his one-time friend, complex, disenchanted former plantation owner and army major Daniel Reno and his hired guns had been performed without ceremony or mourners and Henry Buckle had offered his own brand of apology for his threat to condemn Ethan publicly as a traitor.

'I suppose that in the end you did help to save the president's life,' he said grudgingly. Ethan ignored the offer of a handshake from the mayor. It was time to move on and to leave Clarkston behind for good.

'Not any more, Jonathan.' He looked over the boy's shoulder. Alice Cole stood on the doorstep of her sister's house and waited. Ethan lowered his nephew to the ground. He had a lot of explaining to do before he came to the question that had been troubling him for the three days since he left Clarkston behind.

His brother's widow smiled broadly as he led the young boy up the path towards the house. He hoped that was a good sign and that she would still be smiling when he asked her to marry him.